The Other Side Of The Mirror

The Other Side Of The Mirror

Logan Selling

Have you ever wondered what's on the other side of a mirror?

A world, an island, a dream or, just maybe the exact opposite...

I can't prepare you for what might happen, but I can warn you that you will be taken in by this story and won't be ready for what's around the corner...

You never know what you might find until you've found it, you never know what you might see until you've seen it, and you never know what might happen until its happened.

So get ready for an adventure you can't turn back on...

I had never seen something so magnificent, so majestic, and so wonderful. How had I gotten so lucky to inherit something so amazing?

Grandma's disappearance was a blessing in disguise. Well, uh, it was a very sad event, but it has now been long enough that everything is mine! I had so little to have so much.

No one will ever know how she could afford the 12-bedroom estate that stood before me or how she had gotten away with murder that one time.

It's not as bad as it sounds; don't worry. She just

killed my parents…

Okay. That does sound bad, but it was self-defence! My parents were crazy! Well, that's what Granny told me. I was very young when they died, so I don't really remember anything, but I don't want to, based on what I have been told.

Oh yes, my name is Lucas, by the way. I am 28, and as you can probably tell, I have just received a large inheritance from my long-lost crazy grandma!

Stepping through the door once again after being stolen away over 15 years ago and taken into care was like walking into a ghost house. When she killed my parents all of those years ago, she was taken to a mental hospital, leaving me without a guardian.

Now, although everything she owned was some of the most incredible items you've ever seen, I am forced to sell the whole lot, including the house.

When she was taken away, she couldn't pay her bills, leaving her with loads of debt. Now, with no other options, I must sell everything. The money she had left behind was given to my half-brother, who didn't want anything to do with me.

He and I lost touch when we were sent to different care homes, and now we choose not to talk.

If I had any other choice, I would keep my grandma's house. But sometimes life throws obstacles that you just have to deal with.

I have exactly 2 weeks to clean up and enjoy my time in the house before it goes up for auction, so I must go through all of Granny's old things and explore while I have a chance.

Being back inside the house was one of the eeriest things I've ever had to do; it felt as if I was being watched every step of the way, and I had a sudden chill go down my spine. Steadily, I crept over the old, burnt, blood-red carpet towards one of the most splendid entrances you can imagine! The staircase in front twisted all the way to the top floor, with an incredible chandelier all the way down through the centre, and then to either side of me were some hand-carved archways more unbelievable than I remembered.

The words I use really cannot describe the beauty of this masterpiece. Vines had started to crawl through the windows in all the years of it being abandoned and alone; it added so much character to the house, so much life, but at the end of the day, if I wanted to get it sold for a good price, I would have to tear it down before it was completely overgrown.

To either side of me, through each of the towering archways, it was like a different house... When a building such as this has been left for so long, you really can't expect it to not be vandalised and stolen from, as upsetting as that is. This was my grandmother's life. The garbage torn up over the floor from people littering, the ripped-up photographs everywhere, and nothing valuable left to claim...

Some things in life are just too sad and out of our control.

Thinking to myself now, if I had visited Granny at the mental hospital when I was younger and been there for her more, maybe she wouldn't have gone missing, maybe she could still be home, and me and my brother would still be talking. If only...

I continued through the house, exploring room after room downstairs, and then I decided to go upstairs and take a look up there. It came as a surprise to me that it had been mainly left alone, and not much was broken or stolen, or so I thought.

Thud...

Behind me, a loud noise occurred, leaving me frozen still and with a feeling of utter vulnerability. Someone was here! Trespassers!

"Hello!? Who's there?" I shouted nervously. "Come out now; I'm going to call the police."

Rapidly, my heart began to beat faster and faster,

as if there was a drum playing in my chest. I slowly started backing up, trying not to make any noise. Unknowingly, I got to the stairs and continued backing up without much thought, which evidently didn't end well as I managed to trip and tumble down each step, one by one.

I landed face-first at the bottom of the stairs but didn't hang around long enough to be seen. Without trying to make much noise, I charged straight towards the front door. I turned the handle, and the grand door creaked open. I was out faster than a cheetah. It took me a couple of seconds to catch my breath, but as soon as I could, I reached for my phone out of my pocket and called the police. Now I had to wait until they arrived, knowing that somebody was inside my house!

I sat down on a large rock in the driveway, yet all around me I kept hearing noises, which I thought may have been coming from inside the house, or possibly

I'm just being paranoid. I did feel quite ashamed of myself that I didn't even make it up to the third floor when looking around. If I had looked to see who was actually inside, then possibly they would have left, but now I'll never know...

As I waited, I had the urge to go back inside and try again, but even as I sat there with these thoughts, I knew I would never be brave enough to actually go back in.

"Psst," I heard a voice from behind me.

"Over here," came another from a different direction.

I knew I wasn't being paranoid! There was someone here! I jumped up off the rock and searched around for the voices before answering, "Who's there?! The police are on their way! Don't try anything! I've got a weapon!" I lied, trying to sound intimidating.

During my search for these voices, the police car

pulled up behind me, and a rather raggedy man approached me.

"Officer! Help, there's someone inside!" I said fearfully.

"Well, what do you want me to do about it?" he sneered.

"What do you mean? There's someone in my house or outside, or both; I don't know, but I need your help!" I sobbed.

"Why don't you disappear like your old granny, ay?" he grinned.

"I'm sorry, but who the hell do you think you are?!" I exclaimed.

"The person who helped kill your parents..."

Huh? What did he mean? I felt like being sick! My Granny said it was self-defence! Who was this officer!? How dare he think he can talk to me like that? There's no way...

"What do you mean?" I whispered, trying not to

throw up.

Out of nowhere, the officer pulled out a gun from his jacket pocket and aimed it towards my chest, but before I could even react, **BANG!**

Whoa!

What just happened?! Owwwww... My head, it hurt so much... I don't know what happened, but I had just awoken lying at the bottom of the stairs! I must have knocked myself out when falling. Meaning whoever was in the house before could still be here, and the police still hadn't been called!

You know what! Who the hell do they think they are?! Scaring me out of my own house, making me knock myself out... well, yeah. I'm going back up there! If they didn't leave while I was knocked out, well, that was their first mistake!

"I'm coming back upstairs! If you're still there, I suggest you come out now," I shouted nervously.

I stomped hurriedly up the stairs as ferociously as I

could, trying to scare them. Once I arrived at the top, I didn't waste a second before grabbing a shard of broken glass from an old, broken picture frame. If someone was still here, I wasn't going to let them get away!

I crept silently but swiftly down the corridor towards the room where the sound had come from originally. As much as I wanted to turn back, I didn't. I tried not to think about what I was doing by thinking of that crazy dream I had; it felt too real to be fake. And what he said—killing my parents? I had never met the person, let alone told them about my parents. (Obviously, I know it was just a dream, but I must have met him somewhere.)

When I got to the door that I heard the noise within, I took a second of preparation and then twisted the golden doorknob into what seemed to be Granny's old room. It seemed whoever was here before was gone... OH! It angered me too much! How

STUPID must I be to have let them get away?! If I hadn't been too frightened to begin with, then maybe just maybe I could have caught the ragged crook that was squatting in my grandma's room!

Then I realised at this moment that my wallet and phone were gone from my pockets! Whoever was here must have taken it when I was knocked out! To be honest with you, even though I just arrived, I just want this house gone! Even if I had my phone to call the police, I probably wouldn't; it wouldn't be worth it now.

With the knowledge that no one was here, I decided to continue exploring the rest of the house without feeling the slightest bit worried if someone was still lurking around. Let's just say I still had that shard of glass from the broken picture.

The house was astonishing behind all the graffiti and trash, but it would never be my home. Even though I was only young when I once lived here, it still held too many bad memories.

I got to the top floor, which I soon found out was just a large attic space full of boxes and old pieces of furniture—nothing fancy.

The floors seemed to be rotting through—just another thing I'll have to add to my list of things that need fixing before I can sell. It seemed like there had never been anything renovated in the attic, which was odd as the house was at least 200 years old. At the far end, a huge part of the roof had caved in, blocking whatever lay behind, probably more boxes. It was quite shocking how little had been taken from the attic; to be honest, I don't know if anything had even been taken.

CRRRRRRR... AAASHHHHH...

The rotting floor beneath me began to crash down to the ground, making me go down with it!

Why me...?

Whatever, what a day this has already been. I don't

even feel like moving right now. I think I will sleep this day through and wake up tomorrow, hopefully with a better day ahead.

Goodnight for now...

Well, not the comfiest sleep in the world, but not the worst, surprisingly, considering I slept in old, crumpled boxes and rotting wooden planks.

I stood from the garbage and took myself down the twisting staircase to the kitchen, where I made myself a scrumptious bacon sandwich and a cup of tea with a couple of cheeky biscuits on the side.

Mmmmmmmmmmm. So tasty!

The last mouthful was so delicious yet so depressing, as it meant there was no more left. But anyway, back to reality, and the reality is that everything is hell... I have no money to afford the repairs there are to do; everything I had was in my wallet that was stolen. I should have reported it to the police, but after everything, I just didn't feel up to it. I still technically could, but it's not like I had a lot of money anyway, and I think as long as everything else goes smoothly, I should be okay.

I will have to rummage through all the boxes and see if there is anything worth anything left. Then I've got to get someone to buy it. Otherwise, I won't have any money for the repairs that need to be done.

First, I started by searching the kitchen, as that was where I was anyway. There wasn't much around other than a couple of old plates and cups. A lot of them were smashed all over the floor, but there were a couple. I loaded them up into a box, then went onwards to the main living room. This was the most vandalised room, meaning that most stuff was gone or broken, but not everything. Underneath all the rubble were a few old photo frames that looked to have bits of gold on them! To anyone else, this may look fake, but none of them knew my grandma like I did! She would never own fake gold!

She was too much of a snob to do that.

This was definitely going to get me a few bucks, but I wasn't done yet! There were still loads of rooms to search: the 12 bedrooms, the dining room, all the bathrooms, and last but not least, the massive attic.

In the end, I managed to acquire:

- 2 gold photo frames
- Some old plates and cups
- Grandma's last husband's golf kit
- Some magazines from about 50 years ago

And an old radio. Although this wasn't much, it was something.

Now just to find a good place to sell all these old items, as I can't imagine random people wanting to buy this stuff from me.

I know! I passed an antique store on my way to the house; they would surely buy all this old stuff. Hopefully…

So, on my way I went, I hoped to at least get a couple thousand pounds... My expectations might be a bit high, but the photo frames with the gold within must be worth plenty on their own! If I can't even get that much money, then the house is screwed.

I walked calmly on my way, through fields of cows and streets of shops, until I finally arrived.

At the antique store...

When I walked into the shop, it stunk of tobacco and candles. It wasn't the place I wanted to leave my grandma's things, but I needed the money. Although I won't be getting that money unless I find the shopkeeper.

"Hello? Is anyone here?" I shouted while still trying to be quiet.

"Oh, two seconds. Will be right out," I heard a

rustic voice from a faraway room.

"Okay, thank you," I answered quietly.

I searched around for a while as I was waiting; there were quite a few pictures of Granny's house around, which I didn't find too odd as it was extremely old.

"Oh, hello, sir. Was it you who called?" I heard a voice from behind me.

"Ah, yes, that would be me. I've brought some of my grandmother's old things to sell," I told him.

"Oh yes, what have we got here then? I do have to warn you that we only take the best of the best here," he smirked.

"Well, I think a couple of my items may interest you. May I also say that they are from the old house in the pictures you have here?" I pointed towards the pictures, trying to get a reaction out of him, which I did!

"Oh! Really! Well, let's have a look then!" he said

excitedly.

He searched through the items, giving each item a very interested look, but when he offered me a price, I was astonished!

"Well, all the stuff here looks in good condition, and I don't think I could let you leave here without me having these items! So how about £3,700?"

"Oh my god! Really?" I asked in a surprised voice.

"Yes! This stuff is incredible! I'll have it all off you at once!" he said.

He handed me the money straight in cash, and I was out of there as happy as can be! Although I did wonder why he would pay that much for a few items, but I couldn't care less! And now I had the money for the repairs and a bit extra that I could treat myself with.

The next stop was just next door, and that was the phone store! I am going to get a brand new phone, so that way I can order all the stuff I need for the repairs and whatever else I may want! But which one should I choose? There were three I liked in particular: the Grape X, the SingSong Pro, and the Giggle 5000. They all look so good, but I think the Giggle 5000 is the right choice for me, and it's only £900!!!!!! No, I am going to treat myself! I think I deserve it!

"Hello. Service anyone?" I started shouting around, as I didn't see any employees. "Hello..."

"Ah, yes, how can I help you?" I jumped in fright as the worker asked from behind me.

"Jesus! You scared me!" I yelled.

"Oh, I'm sorry," he giggled.

"I would like to buy the Giggle 5000, please," I asked.

"Of course you can; if you can just give me your details, and I will help you set that up, sir," he offered.

"Okay, thank you," I said.

He helped me set it up, and then I paid him and left feeling extremely happy about my new phone while also embarrassed for getting jump-scared in front of the worker.

It was time for me to head back home now anyway, as I had stuff to do and couldn't be out all day!

I decided to get a taxi home, as that seemed like a nice thing for me to do for myself, as I now have a bit of money so I can afford it, and it will be quite nice to look out around the town and learn my way a bit easier.

Back at the house...

The day doesn't stop here, though; there is still plenty to do, including cleaning up, hiring some builders, and buying supplies for the roof. There are also a couple of pieces of furniture to buy, and then the house will be perfect!

First things first, I got to cleaning up all the old bits of rotten flooring and boxes that had fallen through upstairs, then I ripped off all the old graffiti-covered wallpaper that was painful to look at much longer, and last but not least, I just spent a little bit of time sweeping the floors and wiping down all the surfaces I could to make the house feel a bit more like a home again.

I also called up a building company and arranged for them to come at their earliest convenience with all the supplies that were needed, along with ordering some additional items online.

Everything for the day was done. I had money again. I had a phone again, and best of all, Granny's house seemed like home again.

It had reached that time of night once more, and I felt just too tired to go on. Granny's room held the largest and comfiest of all beds in the whole house, and since I had cleaned it up and changed all the sheets on it during my clean-up, it now seemed perfect for a good night's sleep, much better than rotten flooring and boxes.

When I entered the room, I noticed something I

hadn't noticed when I first went in there: an old sheet covering a large item leaning against the wall. Well, obviously, I'm going to uncover it, so you don't need to get too excited! I'm going to do it in a second. Well, maybe in a bit... Okay...Okay... Here goes... When pulling off the sheet, I felt a wave of dizziness, and I was looking forward to witnessing whatever was underneath!

It was a mirror! (What did you expect?)

The silver masterpiece glared me in the eyes like nothing I had seen before; it was spectacular. But there is another time to appreciate it, as I am so tired...

Good night...

5 hours later...

"Who the hell are you in my bed?!" screeched an old lady's voice.

I jumped up in fear, almost screaming, when I was faced with the mirror at the end of my bed, showing the reflection of Granny! How could this be!?

One blink was all it took... She disappeared.

My heart pounded until it almost felt as if it had stopped.

I jumped up in my pyjamas and ran to the hallway.

"Granny!" I screamed, "Granny, where are you?!"

I searched the whole house from top to bottom with no sign of anyone. Am I going mad?!

How on earth am I going to sleep a wink? I don't know.

I won't be able to think about anything else for the rest of the night, for surely it couldn't have been my grandmother. That's just not possible.

But could it have really been her? She had been missing for years.

Anyway, night again...

A sudden knock on the door woke me with a fright. I don't know how I managed to get back to sleep last night after what happened, but somehow I did.

I jumped out of bed and quickly ran to the bottom of the stairs, trying to hurry so that the person knocking wouldn't leave. I peered through a little peephole in the door to see who it was, and it was the postman with all my stuff! I swiftly swung open the door to greet him.

"Hello, is there a Mr Lucas Widdley here?" he asked in a Scottish accent (yes, my surname is

Widdley, by the way).

"Yes, that would be me. Thank you!" I answered excitedly.

"Okay, well, if you could just sign here, that would be great." He handed me a clipboard for me to sign, and then he signalled to the other driver to unload the pallets full of my items.

"The weather is lovely today, isn't it?" I said trying to make small talk.

"Oh yes, it is. It hasn't been a day like this around these parts in a long time," he replied.

"Ohhhhh, how lucky am I then? This is only my second day in town," I told him.

"Oh yeah, where are you from?" he asked.

"Well, I am from here, but I moved when I was younger, so technically, this isn't my second day back in this town, but instead my second day of holiday in this town, I suppose, if I can call this a holiday," I answered.

"Ah, okay…" he said.

It fell silent for a while after this conversation, so I decided that it would probably be best if I got changed out of my pyjamas and into something a bit more casual. But what to wear… A stripy jumper or a plain jumper, a branded t-shirt or a non-branded t-shirt? I know, I will wear my Aninoos tracksuit with my Neke trainers! That will be perfect.

I ran back down the stairs to bring the stuff in, ready for the builders. I had to be careful, though, to make sure I didn't scruff up my Neke trainers, as I only brought them the other day.

As I brought all this in, I couldn't help but think that I brought too much stuff. But who cares? No one will ever truly know the amount I spent on it all, although I will always know, and let me tell you, it's more than I should have.

Now all that was left to do was wait for the builders that I called yesterday, and once they have arrived, I can get working on putting some of the new pieces of furniture together.

While I waited, I decided it would be cool to have a good look at the old mirror to see if there was maybe a name engraved on it somewhere. It would be quite cool to know the creator of it. There's always history behind something like that, and who knows, it may be worth a fortune.

So back up the winding staircase I went for about the 100th time today and into Granny's room, where the mirror was held. It was probably about time I started calling it my room for a while before it was sold, so I don't feel like I'm staying in someone else's bed, as that's kind of creepy.

Steadily, I went over to the mirror, full of excitement and ready to analyse the creation, yet just as I got close, I heard a van pull up in the driveway, probably the builders. My excitement would have to wait.

So back down the stairs again, which I have to say was getting extremely tiresome; this house could really use an elevator. I answered the door again and greeted the builders with a smile.

"Hey! Are you here for the repairs?" I asked, obviously, knowing they were clearly here for the repairs.

"Yes, clearly, that is us!" he answered viciously.

"Um okay... Well, let me show you where the repairs are needed," I answered.

I had it in mind to tell him to leave on the spot, but I needed the repairs done as soon as possible.

I let them in and showed them to where needed repairs, and I also offered them a cup of tea or coffee, which, of course, is what you are supposed to do for a guest. Anyway, I won't bore you anymore; let's get to the mirror!

I quickly ran over to the mirror and stared myself dead in the eyes. Whoa! I look good today!

Oh... Sorry...

I started searching around the rustic silver frame looking for the name of the creator, and it was just quite a fascinating piece of work.

Knock** *Knock

Oh, the builder must be knocking on the bedroom door... I walked over and opened it, but what I saw was strange—very, very strange!

"MUM!" I screamed.

That's right You heard me right, my mum!

"WHO ARE YOU IN MY MUM'S NEW HOUSE?" she screeched.

"What? Mum, it's me. I have so many questions!" I said excitedly.

"Mum! Mum! Who are you calling mum, and why are you in my MUM'S house!?" she exclaimed.

"Um, what do you mean?"

"This is my mum's house, Patricia... I'm guessing you know her if you're snooping around her room!"

Yes, my grandmother's name is Patricia.

"Patricia is my nan... I'm so confused right now."

"Well, she can't be your nan because that would make you my child, and I don't believe I have any children as far as I know."

"I can't believe you're alive," I said, completely zoning out of the moment.

"What do you mean?" she screeched. "I think it's about time you leave this instant!"

"But..." There's no point in arguing with her; she must have bumped her head or something.

But that means Granny never killed her!

I reached for my phone to call the police, but it was gone! My brand-new phone... How could I have been so stupid as to lose it already? It must be around the house somewhere, as I haven't been anywhere to lose it since I bought it.

"By any chance, do you have a phone I could use?" I hesitated to ask my mum.

"Well, there's a phone box around the corner," she answered, which surprised me that she actually wanted to help me—or so I thought.

"Thanks. Well, I guess I'll be on my way then," I lied to get away quicker.

"Yes, you better hurry; I don't want to keep them waiting!" she answered excitedly.

"Who's waiting? I never told you who I was calling!" I asked, feeling fairly nervous at this point.

"Oh, no one. Sorry. Safe travels!"

Even though I was more confused than the moon being made from watermelon, I quickly walked downstairs and towards the front door.

Who even uses phone boxes anymore?

Before I could reach the front door, I could see through the windows on either side of it; they had called the police themselves! But that wasn't the most concerning part... My dad was standing with them! They are both alive!

How could this be?

I felt a sudden tap on my shoulder; it was my mum. "You didn't think I would just let an intruder leave, did you?"

"What do you mean!? Mum, stop faking! I stuck up with your games! But dad too? What's going on here?" I questioned.

"Police in here!" she yelled.

"What no! Police, it's her you need! She's crazy!" I screeched.

"Sorry, sir, you're going to need to come with me," the police officer told me as he handcuffed my hands together.

"But wait, how did you even call the police?" I asked. "I was talking to you the whole time!"

"The man you call your father, my boyfriend, was in the hallway listening. So when he heard you, he went and called the police from the phone box," she answered, proud of herself.

I just stood in silence and let the police slowly drag me off to the car. I thought it would be best to not bring up anything about their disappearance to the police until we arrive at the station; otherwise, they may just think I'm a bit crazy, and I would have thought they would already know, to be honest.

As I sat there wondering about the world surrounding me, everything just seemed different... No, I mean really different. That's because it was! The Grape Phone Shop was a sweet shop, and the SingSong Phone Shop wasn't even there! The most shocking one was the Giggle Shop. It was the police station we were going to, or at least a small kind of station!

"Officer, isn't this the Giggle Shop?" I questioned confused.

"The Giggle Shop!?" he giggled. "What on earth is a giggle shop?"

"What? Do they store giggles in a jar?" the second

officer laughed.

"Yeah, and I bet there's a deal where if you buy a smile with a jar of giggles, you get half price!" replied the first officer.

"Look, I'm not joking! Don't need to be so rude!" I shrieked.

"Well, look here, kid. This has been the town station since before I was born, so maybe you need to get your act together!" he exclaimed.

I looked at him confused, and as he pulled up to the station, I realised something... There weren't two officers in the car... Just 1...

"Wait, where did the other officer go?" I asked.

"Another officer? I think you're losing it," he answered rudely.

What the hell...

"There was definitely another officer there!" I shouted.

"Don't lose your temper with me! If I say there

wasn't another officer, I mean there wasn't another officer! You got that!" he yelled.

"Yes…" I muttered.

"WHAT WAS THAT?!" he screamed.

"I said yes!" I shouted back.

"Get out of the car!" he shouted as he grabbed my arm and pulled me out.

He dragged me off to the police station, where I was thrown straight into a cell.

Most of my night was spent staring up at the cobweb-covered ceiling, thoughts racing across my mind, wondering what on earth was going on...

The sleep I did get was painful, both physically and mentally. Physically from the rock-hard bed I was forced to sleep on, and mentally from the nightmare I had. It was so real. It made me never want to sleep again in case it came true.

No. More. Tea.

I mean?! What the actual heck! What's the point of living?!

Oh, sorry, right...

Well, when I wasn't thinking about my horrible nightmare, I did have some other thoughts throughout the night, such as...

What if I tried to escape?

What was going on?

How could I have lost my phone already?

Am I homeless now?

And just things like that, but most of all, I have a family now! Although it doesn't seem like they know that yet.

"Oi, cell number 7! You're being released!" yelled an officer to me.

"Me?" I questioned.

"Yes, you! Clearly, I said cell number 7, didn't I now?! Your bail fee has been paid!" he stated.

I could feel the thunder-like beat of my heart in my chest, the pounding headache that echoed throughout me, and the dizziness that was becoming all too overwhelming.

Handcuffs still clung to my wrists as I was escorted out of my cell. I didn't question who paid my bail, even though the thought had crossed my mind. Then I saw who was waiting for me by the door.

"Granny?" I asked, feeling very perplexed.

"Little Lukey!" she squealed.

She remembered me! Finally, someone to talk to! I ran up to her super excitedly before falling flat on my face, which was rather embarrassing.

"You remember me?" I asked with tears filling my eyes as I stood from the footprint-covered ground.

"No! Ha, you really fell for that! No, my daughter told me about some psycho who broke in, and I thought I better check you out," she laughed.

"But you called me little Lukey?" I questioned her sadly.

"Yeah, well, I saw your name was Luke, and I just kind of put the words together," she replied with a devilish smirk on her face.

"So you didn't pay my bail fee?" I asked.

"Me?! No! Hah! You're hilarious. Anyway, I'm done wasting my breath on the likes of you. I better head off before my home gets burgled again." she said sarcastically before walking away. "Although why someone would pay to have you released, I have no idea!"

"So, who paid the fee then?!" I yelled.

"That would be me," came a rather familiar voice.

It was the antique store owner. Why had he paid to release me? He didn't even know me. I don't think.

"You? Why would you help me?" I asked.

"Do you remember?" he questioned.

"Remember? You mean you know who I am?" I asked.

"Well, not exactly, but I know you from my shop," he replied.

"Oh my god?! How did you know I would

remember you? I mean, everyone seems to be lost or broken. I think they may have been drugged," I stated.

"I read about you in the morning newspaper; you're on the front cover!" he said.

He handed me a page of the newspaper he had brought with him, and he most definitely wasn't lying.

The headlines read, *"CRAZY MAN BREAKS INTO AND TERRORISES FAMILY!"*

The description begins with, *'Man appears harmless, but is he really? Police have taken him into custody for questioning; information is limited! He accused the lovely Widdley family of being his parents after breaking into their home. What a maniac!'*

"Hey!" I yelled.

"Okay, no offence. I'm sorry, but we need to leave now."

"Okay, but where are we going? Why did you pay to release me?!"

"I'm taking you to my shop, and the reason for me

releasing you is for me to know and you to find out!”

I followed him out of the police station, and we continued on up the road, yet it did make me wonder why his shop still stood if all the others had changed, but then again, I can't really question anything when I don’t exactly know what’s going on.

It was weird walking down the street, like everyone was watching me without looking at me and judging me without talking about me. The word must have spread that I *broke into my own house* which sounds stupid, but here we are... and yes, I have tried pinching myself to see if I am asleep; I am not. The pinch hurt very much.

Although, on the plus side, at least my family was alive... I may not sound too excited about this, and you would be correct in assuming so. They lied to me, teased me, and acted like they didn’t know me, then sent me to jail!

What is there to be happy about?

What am I doing?!

I am following a strange shopkeeper I have only met once who, for some reason, bailed me out of jail after barely knowing me, and I'm pretty sure he could be some insane serial killer right now! So I think it's best for me to take my chance and run! By run, I mean jogging to the nearest taxi rank, where I will catch a ride to the nearest hotel for the night! I realise I don't have any money on me at this moment in time or my phone, but I will get to that when it comes to it.

Without trying to make it obvious that I was trying to get away, I began to slow down my pace until he was quite a distance away from me. Once I knew I had enough time to run, I did! I charged down the street and across the roads, almost getting hit more than once by several cars. Oh, and I had a change of plans. I had decided to go back to the house. I know... stupid. Right? You might think so, but I just had a certain feeling.

Here's a simple way to put it...

If you had found out your parents had miraculously come back to life and your grandmother was no longer missing, wouldn't you want to be with them?

You don't need to answer because it will always be a yes.

Eventually, I heard the angry shouts of the antique shop guy as he called for me continuously. I was surprised he wasn't chasing after me, but then again, he was a rather chubby one, so understandable.

I reached the walls of Granny's estate and had to stop and think if this was a good idea. No, it's not. But I'm still doing it. When I thought Granny remembered earlier, my heart stopped, my mind was cleared, and I felt like a piece of me was put back into place. The gravel road beneath my feet was lifting me higher and higher towards the front door, and before I knew it, I was knocking.

No answer.

I knocked again.

Still no answer.

I knocked one last and final time.

And yet... still no answer.

I know they're in. I can't see them or hear them, but it's just too quiet. They're hiding. They don't want me to know they're here!

Without a second thought, I reached for the door handle and twisted slowly. *CREEEEEEEK*

"Hello, you don't need to hide... I'm not going to hurt anyone," I shouted.

No one answered.

"Please come out, someone..." I asked.

I heard something fall upstairs, so I charged straight up and asked again, "Hello? I won't hurt you. Just please come out."

Someone crawled out from underneath a bed and stood up; it was my mother.

"Mum... Look, I'm sorry about yesterday, but I need to talk to you," I said.

"Why do you call me mum?" she asked, looking more terrified than if you were being chased by a clown.

"Because you are..." I replied, looking down in sadness.

"But I'm not, and you shouldn't be in my house. You need mental help," she said.

"No! You need mental help! You're meant to be dead!" I shouted in anger.

"Dead! Is that a threat?!" she exclaimed.

"No, I didn't mean it like that, but I thought you were dead for years, and now you're back and acting like you don't know me," I sobbed.

"I don't know you!"

"Well, what about dad? Did he say anything?"

"Dad?! My boyfriend is not your dad! He is just at the store, and he will be back any minute now, so I think it's best you leave."

"No, I'm not leaving until I've got the truth! If you are not dead, then where have you been all these years?"

"I've been right here!"

"You mean before Granny even bought the place?"

"Well, no, clearly not! We used to live in a small house, not too far away, but still. I've never been dead!"

For about 2 minutes, the room was filled with silence as we both awkwardly stared at each other, both confused and fed up. Without trying to be obvious, I looked around the room a bit. Although I was in Granny's room, it felt different. It was newer. But yet, there was a piece you couldn't forget! The Mirror! I turned around to ask my mum if she knew who created it—small talk mainly—but she was gone! She must have run away!

I didn't bother trying to run after her. Instead, I just

went to leave, as I now know that if I want to have a genuine conversation with them, then I've got to be on their side, and my leaving willingly looks better. As I left to the front door, I couldn't help but notice a note on the table. I felt as if I had to read it just in case it was from my mum.

It read:

We tried to get hold of you, but there was no answer, and we also waited around for quite a while, so that will be an extra charge. Here are your expenses:

For repairs: £1500

For the extra time we waited: £250

For not being available when contacted, we will also be asking for an extra £50.

If we do not hear back from you within 2 weeks, then we will be forced to take you to court!

-   The Building Company

I'm not crazy! The builders were here! And I owe

them a lot of money! They were only here for a few hours!

I wasn't going to pay this ridiculous price!

For now, this will become a tomorrow job; today just feels so overwhelming, and I really do need to catch up on some sleep that was lost from last night.

But where to sleep if not at the house?

Possibly I will just take a walk for a while and decide where I sleep on my way; I can't quite think straight right now.

Last night, I decided to sleep on a bench in the local park.

Obviously, not the comfiest night ever, although something very unusual happened... When I was lying on that bench, I felt something in my pocket. It was my phone! It was in my back pocket the whole time! But I'm sure I checked... Oh well, at least I have it again.

Although it was dead (no charge on the phone).

I went to a cafe just next to the park and requested that they charge my phone for me. I got lucky that they already had the right charger. Once it was fully charged up, I would call the builders to pay my fee, but in the meantime, I brought a nice warm tea and a chocolate brownie.

It's weird staring out of a window when you're paying attention to nothing around you. Like, who's looking at you when you're not paying attention, and what family members are appearing back from the dead when you're not paying attention?

Because that is a very common question...

Once I had finished my cup of tea, which was very good by the way, I got my phone back with a 25% battery, which should be plenty to call the builders up, depending on how long I will be arguing with them on the phone.

I looked for their contact information, and once I found it, I thought it would be a good idea to make sure it was a good time to call by sending them a message.

I wrote, "Hello. I got the letter you left yesterday and just had an inquiry about it. I just wanted to ask if it would be a good time to call."

They shortly after replied with a lovely message saying, "If you must."

So, I did…

"Hello," I said in an enthusiastic tone, as that's just the thing you say when you start a conversation.

"Yeah, hi," the guy answered.

"So, I actually wanted to ask a couple of questions, the first one being, why is the bill so extortionate?" I asked.

"Huh?! The bill is what we charge you, not what you choose," he answered rudely.

"Yes, and I understa—" I said.

"Are you going to pay the bill or not?" he demanded.

"No, not until the price is lowered!" I stated.

"That's not going to happen."

"Well then, you're not getting paid."

"Then see you in court."

He hung up

Well, that seemed to go well... I guess my negotiating skills aren't that great. I still had to pay the bill either way, so I rang them back up, and surprisingly, I got an answer...

"So, are you going to pay this time, then?" he asked.

"Yes... But is there any chance I could get it lower?" I asked.

"Ha, ha, ha," he sarcastically laughed.

"It's not that funny," I said.

"Ha, ha, ha," he laughed again.

"Look, I'll pay, okay?"

"Ha, ha, ha. You really are a stupid one, aren't you?"

"I'm sorry?"

"You don't recognise my voice, do you? Ha, ha,

ha."

I had to think for a second, but it didn't take long before I realised the unthinkable...

"You!" I screeched.

"So, I see you've remembered..." he replied.

"Wha... wha... bu... why... how..."

"Stop with the stuttering and just listen here... We will meet soon, and you won't even know it. I can take everything you have and yet give it straight back... Have fun trying to figure that one out."

He hung up

"What?! Hello? Hello?!!!"

It was him. The officer from my nightmare!

I was being stared at all around by people in the cafe. I had completely zoned out when on the phone call, and now it seemed like I was just screaming at someone on the phone, which technically I was.

I had an idea! Maybe my mum would know who that person is. It's still weird to say.

I won't bore you with the journey, but I had decided to go back to the house to talk to my mum once more.

Here are some of my thoughts on the journey:

What if the strange guy is my brother pulling a prank?

I really like tea.

What if I died and this was just my version of hell?

Tea is really good.

But yes, those were some of my thoughts. And now I had arrived at the house.

It was weirder than usual walking up to the door, and I remembered the time I had been shot in my dream. Which wouldn't usually be too creepy, but it was as if I had actually had a call from the dream person... I'm pretty sure that doesn't usually happen.

I let myself into the house, as I had just gotten used to walking in. I probably shouldn't, but oh well.

"Mum!" I shouted, hoping for her to come out.

"Mum!"

Maybe it would be better if I called her by her actual name, as clearly she doesn't like it when I call her mum. Her real name is Tia.

"TIA! TIA! Are you home?" I shouted.

Huh... No answer. I guess they are not in then... Well, I'm still going to look around a bit, as maybe there was something about their disappearance around...

The first place I went was to the kitchen, as I fancied making myself a cup of tea. Then I had a weird thought: How am I going to tell them I'm selling the house? I think it's best to keep that to myself for a while...

I noticed something in the corner of my eye, which Confuzzled my brain a bit.

Confuzzled – Meaning confused in a more fun way

Everything was back! The plates, the picture frames, EVERYTHING!

But how could this be? I sold these… I still have the money from them, and I'm assuming it didn't just appear out of thin air. Unless maybe Granny and my parents brought them, but they haven't been here that long…

Speaking of my family, where could they be?

Unless they're all hiding again…

Knock

Knock

Knock

Someone was at the door. Maybe it could be Granny or someone, although I'm pretty sure they wouldn't knock on their own door.

I went over and peeped out one of the side windows, trying not to be seen. It was the builders! I'm not answering them… Not after that phone call. What if that person from my nightmare was there? I couldn't quite see everyone; I don't know if that person was there!

Knock

Knock

Knock

They began knocking louder and, for some reason, wouldn't just leave. My only option is to answer. I mean, it should be okay. Shouldn't it?

"Hello... I wasn't expecting you back here this soon," I stated.

"Well, do you not want the job finished?" he questioned.

"Did you not finish yesterday?" I asked, confused.

"What? All that work in one day? Ha. You must be joking," they all began to laugh.

I chuckled along with them, confused as anything.

"But why did you leave a bill then?" I asked.

"A bill? We didn't leave a bill," he stated.

"I must be losing my mind... Wait, actually, I have it on me." I said this while reaching into my pocket. But where is it? It's gone... "I'm sure I have it here somewhere…”

"Look, bill or no bill, it wasn't from us! So can we finish our work or what?!”

“Um, I suppose, but I could have sworn that you said it was finished.”

“Well, it's not, so we are going to go and get our work done, and it seems like you may need to sit down.”

I nodded politely and let them in; he was right. I do need to sit down… The paper was in my back pocket the last time I checked. I must have lost it on the bench last night or possibly in the café this morning…

The builders came in one at a time, bringing in all their tools and construction items. They must have thought they were being funny by dragging in mud all over the carpets!

You know, I may just have a little nap… (This is where the screen fades black in movies.)

3 hours passed…

Another 3 hours passed...

And you guessed it... Another 3 hours passed...

I slept for 9 HOURS!

I was eventually awoken at 11 pm by a leaving builder. They stayed quite late, surprisingly.

"Oh my god! Sorry, I didn't mean to sleep for so long! What are you even still doing here? You know what? I don't really care, and thank you for waking me," I said quickly, as he had made me jump a bit.

"Um, okay, goodbye," he answered with a scared look on his face.

I got up and shut the door behind him, feeling absolutely astonished that I slept for so long, yet I still felt tired!

"Mum, Dad… Granny!" I shouted, trying to find out if they were home just yet.

Still no answer… It's odd that they aren't back yet. I hope they're okay.

Since it was already quite late in the evening and I

already felt exhausted, I went up to Granny's room to sleep for the night. It was the only room in the whole house that was clean and fully furnished, so it was really the only possible place I would feel comfortable sleeping in for the night. If they did return home at some point in the night, then I would, of course, find somewhere else to go, as I know they would not be okay with me staying, but for now, I choose comfort.

I walked up the stairs towards Granny's room once more. I know, crazy, right?! But before I twisted the doorknob, I could hear someone breathing inside. Maybe I was wrong; maybe my family was back... In that case, this is going to be very awkward.

I opened the door and walked in. I was right. Granny was home! And sleeping in her bed... I mean, I know I don't technically live here now, but I just want a warm bed tonight. I think that one night on a bench in the park was enough for me.

Unexpectedly, she turned her head and gave me a

death stare, like she was looking into my soul. She didn't say anything; she just stared at me for about 5 minutes straight, and I didn't know what to do.

"You..." she mumbled with what sounded to be the sorest throat I had ever heard, "You..."

"Sorry... I can leave," I said, trying not to anger her.

"You killed her!" she shouted, "YOU KILLED HER! *You killed my daughter!*"

My face froze in fear, my hands trembled, and I felt like I was falling into space from the ground to Mars. I know that makes no sense, as that is how I felt.

"What do you mean?" I stuttered.

"AHHHHHHHHHHHHHHGHGHGHGGHHGAHAH HHAHHHHGHGHG" she bellowed.

Like your nightmares and the scariest horror movies, what happened next is too much to explain.

Almost as if her legs were grabbed from the end of her bed, she shot out and straight through the mirror in a puff of grey, cloudy smoke!

WOAH!

WHAT HAPPENED?! I woke up with a jolt, and once again, it was a dream. These dreams were becoming torturous!

I was still on the sofa. I must have fallen back to sleep after the builder woke me up.

It had officially passed 3 am at the time of my waking up, meaning there were only 9 days left until the auction, and I had to find a way to tell my family. I could just cancel the auction, but it's MY inheritance! Whether they're dead or not.

On another note, I do actually need to find them. The last thing I want is for them to go missing again. Now didn't feel like the best time to go looking though due to it being 3 am and being pitch black outside, with nothing but the street lights to guide the way. Yet I didn't feel tired. Maybe a peaceful walk in the park would be nice.

So I put on my shoes and coat, then off I went, walking past all the garbage around every corner, graffiti covering every wall, and I could go on. You really notice these things at night when no one is around.

All of a sudden, I heard a quiet whining sound coming from behind a bush. I thought I was going crazy, so at first I ignored it and continued walking, but yet the noise just wouldn't go away, so I turned back and went towards the bush to have a look at what might be hiding.

IT WAS A DOG!!!

A puppy. He was just lying behind the bush, crying out for someone to find him. I didn't know whether or not I was supposed to take him or just let him find his own way home. Then again, he looked all too innocent and timid to be left alone. Honestly, he was adorable, to say the least—completely brown all over, white belly and paws, and the ears—oh my god, they were the silkiest, most soft and fluffy ears I had ever felt.

For now, I'm going to call him Chip!

I picked him up off the ground and carried him along with me through the park. The stars glistened in the sky, the wind blew through the trees, and everything seemed so perfect in the night light. I think having a pet with me for a while could be the one good thing going for me at the moment.

After some time, he fell asleep in my arms, and I took a seat on the grass with him as calmly as possible. I think watching him in total silence, just relaxing, made me begin to feel rather sleepy myself, which I don't really know how was possible after how long I'd slept!

Eventually, I did fall asleep outside on the grass and was awoken by the sudden yelping sound of Chip! I began to freak out, searching around until I caught a glimpse of him in the corner of my eye as I witnessed a thug dragging him away! I jumped up from the ground and stopped breathless in the moment. It was him. You know who. The creepy guy from my nightmares! Except this time, I didn't wake up. He was here. I was here. What to do?

"Oi! Let go of my dog!" I shouted.

The man almost jumped off his feet as I alerted him and, in a panic, threw Chip to the side, then darted off down the street! I ran over to Chip as fast as possible to make sure he was okay, and instantly my reaction was to get back up and chase after the man, yet I didn't quite see the direction he went in, and I wasn't prepared for a wild goose chase around town.

Why won't this man just disappear!? Leave me alone!

And what did he want with Chip!?

I have so many questions that need answering, so many thoughts that I need time to think through, and just a ticking clock that won't stop in my head as I count the days that I have left before I sell the house and leave this town! Right now, I just need to get out of this park! I should never have fallen asleep in the first place, especially considering the park was full of people now and the large clock in the centre stated the time as 11 am. I had wasted half a day!

Well, not to waste any more time; straight to what needs to be done! Chip is probably quite hungry and will be in need of food soon. I suppose I could start my day off by heading to the local pet store before I make my way home. Then I can get him a few bits, such as a bed, food, toys, etc...

The pet store was a very large building that took pride in its spot directly across from the park; it was like an animal theme park! Being in this location was great for me, as it meant I really didn't have far to go, so I quickly ran over and was there in seconds.

I got straight to looking for what I needed and

chose the fluffiest bed I could find, the most fun toys for him, and then, the most expensive food... oh, well, when you see the most expensive food there costs £237.49, then you might go for a bit of a cheaper bag... The one I ended up picking up cost £37.09, so it was still pricey but not the most expensive. In total, my price came to:

Price List:

. *£37.09 – Dog Food*

. *£26.28 – Dog Toys*

. *£89.00 – Dog Bed*

-Total £152.37

Quite expensive, but all worth it for my new little pup. I decided that once I got all these items, instead of heading straight home, I would go and see the Antique Shop Guy. I felt I needed to apologise for running off before and possibly offer some of the money back for my bail. Well, we'll see about that one later.

His shop was only a couple of miles away from me and wouldn't take an overly long amount of time to arrive at, especially with Chip accompanying me the whole way.

When I head home afterwards, I do hope my family has returned, as it's been quite a while since I last saw them. Who knows? Perhaps they're missing again! Wouldn't that be hilarious? Ha, no, okay, sorry.

Although it will be nice to see my family and have Chip with me, it all seems so perfect. All I could hope for now was for my brother to talk to me again. You know what? I'm going to call him! I still remember his number! Whether he answers or not is another question, but I can only try...

Ring...

    Ring...

        Ring...

As I heard my brother's voice when he answered

the phone, I suddenly felt lost for words. A measly "Hello" left my mouth, and I eagerly awaited for his reply.

"Hey. Who's this?" he asked.

Without much thought and a feeling of excitement, I replied, "Um, Ah, Smith..." Why on earth did I choose that name? I don't know.

"Okay... Hi, Smith. Can I help you with something? Do I know you?" he asked.

"Well, you do, but... Okay, this might sound crazy. I just need you to trust me on this one. In fact, if you were free tomorrow by chance, would you be able to meet me at your childhood care home? I can explain everything there," I replied.

"I'm sorry, but I don't know anyone by the name of Smith," he stated anxiously, "how do you even know I was in care or where the care home was?!"

"They're alive, Joe," I sobbed.

"Right, I don't know what you're talking about..."

he said angrily, "Is this some kind of joke!?"

"Please stop shouting," I asked with tears rolling down my cheek.

"Stop shouting! Don't you tell me to stop shouting when you're the one who's talking about my family! They're dead, and my grandmother is missing! Are you saying you know where she is? Spit it out, won't you!?" he shouted.

"Look, I know this all sounds crazy, but I just need you to take a chance... Just be at your care home at 1 pm tomorrow. I'll explain everything then." I hung up the phone and burst into tears in the middle of the street. I felt like screaming a tornado into existence. You don't know the feeling of hearing his voice.

The tears were of joy, and I couldn't be happier, although Joe would soon realise who I really am, not Smith, of course. And I didn't even know how to get to his old care home! It was just the first place I thought of on the spot.

How could I find out? Actually, the antique guy had all of those pictures of the house around; maybe he had some information about everything that happened with my family when I was younger. And where Joe's care home was.

Something odd I noticed while on the move was that the phone shops were back! The Grape phone shop is the Grape phone shop, and the Giggle phone shop is a Giggle phone shop again! Even the SingSong shop was back to normal! *HUH*… I think I must be losing my mind. The police station must have been on another street; I must be getting it mixed up.

"Well, Well, Well, look who it is," the antique man tapped me on the shoulder from behind.

"Oh… I was just coming to see you. Look about me running off last time," I said.

"Save it. I have nothing to say to you," he sighed.

"Look, please, I really need your help," I begged.

"What could you possibly need from me? I was

there when you got yourself locked up, and you straight up left me! I have nothing to say to you!" he exclaimed.

"I need to find out where my brother's childhood care home was... I hoped you might have some information for me. I mean, you have all those pictures of our house. I just thought you might know some history."

"I do. But you can think again if you think I'm going to tell you anything," he stated.

He barged past me and into his shop, trying to ignore my every action. I kept trying to convince him to help me, but he wasn't having any of it! I didn't know what to do.

Suddenly, he turned to me and asked, "Where did you get that dog?"

"I found him in the park," I replied.

"I need to show you something important," he said.

He walked me over to a room out the back of his shop and showed me pictures of the mirror in Granny's room.

"What's this?" I asked, "This isn't what I asked for."

"A mirror," he replied sarcastically.

"Well, duh… But why are you showing it to me? I've already seen it multiple times in person. I have no interest in it; I just want to know what I came here for—my brother's care home! The only thing I have ever cared for about that mirror is whoever created it; I mean, it is incredible," I said.

"Me. I made it," he stated.

I couldn't believe that he created that masterpiece and couldn't hold back my reaction, "What?! You did?! It's a really nice mirror!"

"Can you keep a secret?" he asked.

"Um, yes, I suppose. Unless you're about to tell me, you killed someone," I said, trying to be funny.

He took a sigh, and then I couldn't tell if he was being sarcastic, but he told me, "It's powerful. Like really powerful…"

"The mirror is powerful." I burst out laughing at him. "It's just a mirror. It's not like my reflection is going to walk out!"

"You would be surprised," he snickered.

"Do you think you're being funny?! You know what? I don't even know why I bothered coming here," I said, turning around to leave.

He laid his hand on my shoulder and yelled, "Listen! Just stay away from the mirror!"

I let out a light giggle, knowing it would annoy him, then left to obviously go straight to the mirror, as that's what you do when someone tells you not to…

I was still no closer to finding out where my brother's care home was, but maybe Granny might know if I could find her. If she can actually remember anything.

Or if all fails, then what do I do!? If my brother turns up and I'm not there, it may be my only shot at talking to him. But wait! What if there's post or something at the house that might lead me to the address?

I rushed back home and burst through the front door. No one else was there, so I got straight to searching everywhere—the floors, the draws, even under Chip's paws—but I was coming up with nothing.

Possibly I could have put it somewhere earlier when I cleaned the house. But where!?

What if I accidentally threw it away?

No, surely not...

Surely even I would have looked at the post before just throwing it out. So again, I got to looking around all downstairs, upstairs, hallway to hallway, and each and every room, which led me to end up in Granny's room. There it lay. On the floor in front of the grand mirror... The mirror I was told not to go near. How very odd. But I'm sure it's fine... Slowly, as I walked towards it, a feeling of slight anxiety swirled around me. I leaned over and picked up the letter, turned around, and walked out of the room. Okay, I also gave myself a wave in the mirror just for the fun of it.

I know I'm weird, but whatever, my life, my rules. Calmly, I wandered back down the stairs towards the sofa, where I opened the letter revealing the address and phone number for the care home. Now just to make a quick call to the care home to make sure the address was right on the letter, but when I got downstairs, they were back!

"You, there. My daughter told me about you. Breaking in again. Harassing her!" shouted my grandmother.

"What no! I just tried talking to her! Look, I'm going to have proof that you're my grandmother very soon!" I stated.

"Oh really? And how are you planning on doing that?" she questioned.

"My brother. I'm meeting him tomorrow, and he'll tell you I'm not crazy!"

She lifted one eyebrow and towered over me before saying, "Can I tell you something, child?"

"I'm 28 and not a child, but yes, what do you have to tell me?" I replied.

"I believe you. I don't think you're crazy, but I can also tell you that my daughter doesn't have a child. I understand you're genuinely serious about what you're saying," she said.

"That doesn't make me feel much better, or really make much sense, but thanks... Where have you guys all been lately anyway? I haven't seen you around," I asked.

"We've been right here... I don't really leave the house these days, so I'm always here," she explained.

"Well, that can't be, as I have been here as well and

haven't seen you once," I stated.

"I'm not lying, child, and why have you been in my house anyway?!" she questioned me angrily.

"STOP CALLING ME, CHILD! My name is Lucas! And if you let me explain the situation, then you would know why I've been here!" I shouted.

"Okay, no need to shout. I'll go put the kettle on and make us a brew, then you can sit and explain. Okay?"

"Oooh, I do love a good tea!"

"Hey, maybe we are related!" we laughed.

She went off to make the tea, and I felt so confused again. I just don't know what's going on anymore. This wasn't what I expected when inheriting the house.

When she came back with the tea, she had made a whole pot, making me think this conversation was going to be longer than I had originally thought.

"Ah, that's a lot of tea," I spoke.

"Not too much, though, am I right?" she chuckled, seeming to be in a much better mood.

"Never!" I laughed.

A sudden chill filled the room, and all fell silent. I wanted to get up, leave, and go home, but this sort of was my home.

"Basically," I said, "You killed my parents; you were taken to a mental hospital, which you escaped from and went missing for many years to the point that I inherited this house we are in now, and my brother inherited all your money. Now suddenly, you're back like nothing has happened and my parents are alive... You know what? I think I am going crazy!"

"Follow me," she replied.

"I just say all this to you, and that's all you have to say!" I exclaimed.

"Just follow me," she repeated.

I followed her up the stairs and into her bedroom.

"Goodbye, Lucas," she sobbed.

"What do you mean?! Goodbye… Are you going to kill me?!" I exclaimed.

"Just know I miss you more than you will ever know. Tell your brother I am so proud of both of you. I don't know if I'll see you again, but just know I'm with my family, and I can't live without them again. The truth will come out, I promise you. Goodbye"

She slammed the door shut and locked me in. I was trapped. I stood still without reacting to anything. Tears filled my eyes. What did she mean? What is the truth? What even just happened? It all went so quickly…

I went and sat on her bed, and I was greeted by myself in the reflection of the mirror. You know what I'm locked in here. I might as well have a look at the mirror now and see its powerfulness. But just as I expected, it was pretty basic—nothing magical. It was a marvellous mirror, but nothing special. Well, that clears that up.

OH! I almost forgot. I've got to meet my brother tomorrow! I needed to get out of this room; who knows how long she planned to keep me locked in here? I ran over to the door to try and force it open, but... Wait, what? The door was unlocked. But she definitely locked it. I don't even care anymore! Where is she?

WHHHAAAAAT! Chip! What happened to him? He was big and older! But you could tell it was him. I just know, but how? He was like 3 months old before, and now he looked at least 6 years old! I'm lost for words.

My little puppy, Chipster, is not a puppy anymore... He looked to of aged six years in a day. I should have left him in the bush and not dragged him into my crazy life.

How is this even possible?!

I don't even care about looking for Granny. She

just locked me in a room, so I have no need to talk to her right now! Even though I know I can get out of her room, as apparently she didn't lock it properly, I'm going to stay here and sleep! I've got a nice, comfortable bed to sleep in, and I'm going to enjoy it!

I never even called the care home, but I'm just going to trust the process and hope I've got the right address. My mind is too conjumbled.

Conjumbled – A word meaning mixed up and confused.

It hadn't taken me long to fall asleep after everything yesterday; I kind of just passed out.

This morning I didn't have any time to waste as I had a train to catch in two hours to meet my brother, but there was still time for a morning tea and biscuits.

I didn't see any more of my family around, which was odd, but to be honest, I didn't expect to. What Granny had said to me burned a hole through me. It's like she was saying goodbye forever. Again.

But anyway, enough of that... You've just listened to all of that already!

I need to get to the train station. And obviously, I can't leave without Chip, my newly born adult dog. Let me put it this way: if you had a dog that was a tiny little puppy, then what would you do if you woke up the next day and it was triple the size? Just think about that for a couple of seconds.

I put his lead on, which was luckily adjustable; otherwise, it most definitely would not have fit him, and then I left the house to go and see my brother. Hopefully, he shows up. He does think I'm called Smith. Although if I got a random call from a random guy called Smith, I don't know if I would turn up to be honest with you.

I left and walked around the corner towards the bus stop. You will never guess who was there! The antique shop guy! What was he doing here? I walked over and sat next to him on the bus stop bench, waiting for him to say something, but he didn't. Eventually, once the bus pulled up, we finally spoke to each other.

"After you," I said, letting him onto the bus first.

That was it. That's all we said. I know exciting, right?

"Look, I'm not sitting on an hour-long bus journey to a 2-hour-long train journey without saying one word! So please just talk to me," I asked.

"I don't know what you want me to say, Lucas. You haven't even… you haven't even apologised!" he shouted in the middle of the bus.

"Will you keep it down back there, or you're going to have to get off!" The bus driver shouted.

"Sorry!" I shouted to the driver.

"Okay, look, I don't know why you think you deserve an apology, but you're not going to find one here," I said quietly to the antique guy.

"I just want you to say sorry for not believing me. I want you to say that you shouldn't have run after I paid for your bail fee. I want you to say..." he whimpered before I interrupted him.

"I'm not going to say any of that because I left to see my family, who were supposed to be dead! I found out they were alive, and I wasn't going to waste a moment without them! You want your money for the bail fee back; I don't have it!" I stated.

"Your family is dead! If you would just listen to me for once! I don't care about the bail money! I'm trying to help you! There are things you don't know," he exclaimed.

"HA," I laughed. "My family is alive and well. I spoke to my Granny just last night."

"Oh yeah? And what did she say to you?"

"Well, um"

"Exactly, not great, I'm guessing!"

"She made me a cup of tea, then we had a conversation."

"That's all?"

"Yeah… well… No, that's all," I sighed.

"No, it's not. Tell me what was said!"

"If you must know then, I explained that I hadn't seen her in years, and she acted like she had never been missing... Then she locked me in her bedroom. Well, I thought I was locked in. It turns out the door was open."

"That's all?"

"No... She told me that she was sorry, and she was proud of us, and she wished she could come back or something, but I can't really remember."

"When you say... us, who do you mean?"

"Me and my brother..." I stated.

"Have you spoken to any of your other family members?" he asked.

"Just my mum, but she didn't say very much."

"What did she say? I need all the facts."

"She didn't say much other than she doesn't remember who I am and claims to have no children, which is what my Granny started like, but I'm pretty sure she remembers now." I said, "What is it to you anyway!?"

"Nothing. Never mind," he saddened.

He went silent, and the rest of the journey was just awkward and lonely. Then came my stop, which also seemed to be his.

"Oh, you're off at the same stop as me. Whereabouts are you heading?" I asked.

"I wasn't going to say anything, but I am going to go and see your brother... I contacted him about, well, that's not your business," he replied.

"Um okay... I'm going there too. Although he thinks my name is Smith," I said.

"Well, he's going to get a surprise, then won't he?" he stated.

"Yeah, probably I sighed. "Well, since I'm assuming I'll keep running into you, what's your name?" I asked.

"It's Julian," he replied.

"Ah, okay," I said.

"Just one more quick question: how many years ago did your grandma go missing?" he questioned.

"Why does that matter?"

"Just answer my question, please!"

"Well, I think it was about fourteen years ago."

"Fourteen years!"

"Yeah, I know, crazy, right?"

I think I had the wrong reaction because he looked dead—breathless, cold, and completely still...

"I had no idea it had been so long... I think I need to tell you something, whether or not you will believe me," he said with an anxious look on his face.

"If this is about that mirror again..." I said with a sigh.

"It is, but if you would just let me explain..."

"No! I've heard enough about that stupid mirror."

"But there is just something you need to know."

"I'm not interested in anything you have to say about that mirror. To be honest, I didn't want to say anything before, but I don't believe you created that mirror, as it looks more than a hundred years old, and I know you're old, but not that old."

"I don't know whether I should be insulted, annoyed, or angry. I'm going to walk on my own now."

He moved away from me and went to stand as far as possible, and to be honest, I don't really care. He's a liar and a freak. I mean, he must be at least 70 years old; does he not have better things to do than make up fairy tales?

This conversation went on our journey to the station, which we eventually arrived at after Julian's tantrum.

When the train pulled up, I got on and ended up taking a nap, as there was nothing much else I could do unless I just sat playing games on my phone, but even that would get boring after a while. I slept for about 45 minutes and spent the rest of the journey sitting with my thoughts. The worst thing you can do is sit with your thoughts.

When the train finally pulled up to my station, I felt relieved for some reason, like a weight had been lifted off my shoulders.

I took a large step off the train, making sure not to fall down the terrifying gap between the train and the platform, which is when I caught a sudden glimpse of Julian again as a weird thought entered my mind: what if I had been asleep for longer and almost missed my stop? Would he have woken me up? Probably not.

A random but genuine question...

I was peacefully on my way to exit the station before someone grabbed me and wouldn't let go! I began to tug away, trying to get free of their grasp, and then I noticed who it was. Joe...my brother.

A tear dropped from my eye to the ground in happiness. I grabbed hold of him and hugged him like I had never before. I hadn't seen him in years; this moment felt unreal. Well, it did until I got shoved away!

"What are you doing here, Luke?! Or should I say, Smith? I told you I never wanted to see you again!" he yelled.

"But…" I whimpered.

"No! When someone says they don't want to see you again, it means they don't want to see you ever again," he shouted.

"But Mum, Dad, and Granny are all alive!" I sobbed.

"No, they're not! It's literally impossible! Mum and Dad were killed! And Granny is presumed dead; otherwise, I wouldn't have all the money I have now, and you wouldn't have your house!"

"Is that really why you won't believe me?! Because you don't want to lose your money!"

"No, of course not! Look, you wouldn't understand! I just don't want to see you anymore. Our family is dead; I just need to move on."

"If they are dead, then I must be going crazy, as I have been having full conversations with them!"

"Do you need money or something? Is that why you're doing this to me?! Making up all these lies!"

"No! Why won't you just believe me? I don't care about your money!"

He stomped off down the road, and in all honesty, I just let him go. I know I'll be able to find him if I need him. Besides, I know Julian's got to meet him soon, so if I hang around the station, then he's bound to turn back up.

In the meantime, I waited in the station café and got myself a cup of tea. I sat in a window seat to get a good view of who was coming. Yet the first person I recognised who came up to the café was Julian! Of course.

He looked me in the eyes as he walked through the door with a look of fright and stated, "I need to tell you something. You might not believe me, but I just need you to hear me out and not push what I say aside. Please, it won't take too long."

"Oh, what!? I'm sick of your face!" I shouted.

"I already told you that I needed to explain something to you," he said.

"Okay. You've got 5 minutes. Go," I scoffed.

"I believe you. Everything you've said is true! Your family is alive, just not the way you think." I stated, "It's another world beyond what we see."

"Okay… okay… I've heard enough. I thought you were going to be serious," I sighed.

"I am! Yes, your family is dead, but they also aren't! It's difficult to explain," he said.

"I give up! Why do I bother listening to you every time!? I'm not crazy, Julian; I don't just believe everything I hear. Don't treat me in such a way." I said angrily. "Please just go!"

"Well, I'm kind of meeting your brother here, so

I'm going to be staying," he said.

"Again, why are you meeting my brother?" I asked.

"I'm not going to tell you anything," he stated.

"Okay, but how do you even know my brother then?"

"I have a history with your family. That's all you're going to get! Now enough questions!"

"But why do you need to talk to him?! None of this makes sense!?"

"Just about stuff, okay?! Now enough!"

"No, not okay! What aren't you telling me?!"

"You know what I'll leave. I'll just wait for Joe outside."

"NO! You will stay right here and explain to me why you need to talk to my brother!"

"Look, I barely know you! We only met a few days ago, and to be quite honest, they have been some of the most difficult days of my life! So, I will only tell you what I want to tell you and nothing more! You got that!?" he snarled.

"No! You're not my parent; you don't get to lie to me and treat me like nothing. I'm selling that nothing-but-trouble house in just over a week, and I can't wait to move me and my family as far away from that town and you as possible!"

My brother walked in through all the shouting and yelled, "will you both be quiet?! People are looking over!"

To be honest, my head was hurting a bit, and for a split moment, I was hoping to wake up from a dream again.

"So, what's all this about then!?" Joe questioned.

"This dimbo won't just let me keep my business to myself!" Julian exclaimed.

Dimbo – A word meaning idiot, stupid, and just pretty annoying

"Well, if you weren't so secretive, then maybe we

wouldn't be having this problem right now!" I shouted.

"I'm sorry, but I'm going to have to ask you to leave," a waiter from the café asked.

"I'd be more than happy to!" I said in anger as I got up and walked away.

"Hey, wait up!" I heard Joe shout at me.

"What! You're the one who stormed away from me before! And now you're friends with this random guy who's apparently got secrets about our family! What is going on, Joe?" I shouted in anger, "I can't keep up with everything anymore!"

"Look, I had a thought, and we do need to have a proper conversation. But that's just not possible right here, right now. Julian has something he needs to tell me in private and some matters we need to discuss. I'll talk to you soon. Just meet me at the café again in about an hour," he said.

"Just answer my question! How do you know

him?" I asked again.

"Lucas, stop! I'll talk to you later!" he stated.

"Just tell me everything, now!" I yelled.

"Just meet me here in an hour, Lucas!"

"Whatever!" I walked away towards... I don't know... anywhere. I had Chip by my side, and that's all I needed.

I ended up just walking from street to street, still getting used to Chip being a lot bigger, but there must be some logical reason why this has happened. I mean, maybe I am in one big, giant dream... or dead... But either way, I've got to live my life.

Along my walk, I passed a quaint-looking bed and breakfast, which I thought would be perfect to spend the night in. Plus, it allowed pets, so that's a perk. I still had to go and meet Joe again in a bit, but at least I had somewhere to storm off to if I needed to.

At least for now, I can just relax for a while and maybe watch a short movie. But what to watch...

There's never anything good to watch anymore; everything is either a remake of an old movie or has terrible acting! I got to the point where I literally couldn't find anything, so I gave up and read a book from the four choices they gave me. I got quite into it and ended up going over time, but hey, I've had to wait what feels like a lifetime to hear from Joe, so he can wait ten extra minutes.

I left Chip back at the BnB so he wouldn't keep getting dragged around with me and could have a rest, then headed back towards the café again. Hopefully, they let me in after being kicked out previously.

It was only about fifteen minutes up the road and around a couple of corners to get back to the café, so I was there in almost no time.

"Julian!" I exclaimed from outside the window.

He still sat at a table with Joe! This was meant to be a conversation between me and my brother!

I stormed through the door and over to the table

they were sitting at before questioning them, "so, what's going on here then?!"

"What do you mean?" Joe asked.

"Well, why is he here?!" I inquired.

"Because we are having a conversation, and he has every right to be here! You don't rule the world!" Joe shouted at me.

"Why do I bother?" I instantly turned around and walked out the door, but was chased after by my brother once again.

"Hey! Stop acting so childish and act your age!" Joe shouted.

"Don't talk to me about acting my age! Maybe if you just listened instead of always having to be right, then we would be able to get somewhere!"

"You know what!? Do you really want to know what we were talking about inside? We were talking about getting you locked away in a mental hospital! Our family is dead, and I know that because I watched you kill our parents."

"Wait… I did what? But Granny killed our parents. Why would you even say that?!"

"Look, it's true, okay!? You killed them, and Granny took the blame! I watched you do it!"

How could this be? I had no memory of this. It couldn't be true. Surely he must be lying!

"I don't believe you!" I shouted.

"Yes, you do! You don't know why you believe me, but you do! There's a piece inside of you that you don't know why is there, but it is, and you know I am telling you the truth!" he screamed at me.

"But it can't be. I only spoke to them the other day," I fell to my knees in despair and hatred towards myself.

Maybe I am crazy.

"This is why we were looking into mental hospitals for you. You physically cannot have spoken to our parents. If you had said just Granny, then maybe there would have been a little bit inside of me that believed you, as she was never found dead, but our parents too. It's just not possible."

"Hey, I didn't want to interrupt you just in case, but I thought now would be a good time," Julian said.

"It's not, Julian," Joe said.

"No, it's not!" I said, standing up from the ground with a face of anger.

"Okay, look, I'm not here to argue. Let's just talk," Julian said.

Without a second thought, I slapped his face as hard as I possibly could, knocking him to the ground.

"I'm not here to argue, but you dare try talking to my family about putting me in a mental hospital again, and you won't just get a slap. I will kill you! Apparently, I've done it before, so I can just as easily do it again with no guilt!" I smirked.

"You mean you killed your parents? I know. But you don't listen to me, so there was no reason to bother explaining it to you," Julian stated.

"You knew this whole time and are only now telling me! To be honest, I didn't expect much more from you. I've barely known you for a week! I don't even care how you know," I said.

"Okay… Okay… Break it up, you two!" Joe exclaimed.

"I'm heading to my B&B now anyway. I'll call you in the morning, Joe," I said before walking away.

There's so much to comprehend, and I still don't completely believe Joe. He was always an attention-seeking pig; he probably killed our parents himself for the attention!

I eventually fell asleep last night with a struggle, but I had strange dreams that almost felt real, but probably because of the whole, I murdered my parents' thing. Although there was one good dream in it all—that I never had to inherit my Granny's house—before I got that house, I rented a nice apartment in the city and had a good job earning a reasonable amount of money. Things were better back then. But either way, I'm here now, and nothing can change that.

I suppose now that I have spoken to my brother, I don't need to hang around anymore. I could head home and continue getting ready to sell the house. But not alone. I want Joe to come back with me and experience the house with me, and I don't know... but... well, I still can't shake off the fact that I have been talking to my family this whole time! If only he could see them! I could prove I'm not a murder-crazy man.

Before any of that could be done, though, I still had to go out for a nice hot cup of tea with Chip. Well, he won't be getting tea, but maybe a cheeky ice cream.

I left the BnB and went on my way towards a park. I hoped there would be a food van or something that I could get tea from and space for Chip to run around.

This town is a lot nicer than the one I'm currently living in; there's no graffiti everywhere (well, not as much), smashed bottles don't cover the streets (well, not as many), and everyone that walks past says hello to you (well, most of them).

My phone began to ring in my pocket

"Hello," I said, in a good mood.

"Hey, Luke. Whereabouts are you?" a voice answered.

"Um, who's this?" I asked.

"Oh, my god. You come all this way to see me, and you don't even recognise my voice," Joe replied.

"Oh Sorry. My mind is just a bit conjumbled. I'm just looking around for a park to hopefully buy a tea and take Chip for a walk," I apologised.

"A park? This isn't that kind of area," he announced.

"What do you mean? It's a park?"

"Yeah, but most of the parks that used to be around are now apartment buildings or shopping centres."

"Oh, okay, so where can I get a tea?"

"Well, if you don't want tea from the café, then I would suggest the train station food van is your best bet... I can meet you there."

"Yeah, that sounds good. I'll meet you there."

I hung up

No parks?! What a weird town this is... I take it all back about it being better than my town! Poor little Chip can't even go for a walk. But at least I will be able to ask my brother about coming with me.

Once I had arrived at the station, I felt blessed to see all the food vans and coffee stations around— plenty of places to grab a cup of tea. It wasn't long after arriving that I saw Joe walk in and wave to me with a cheerful smile on his face.

"Hey. What are you so happy about today?" I asked, "last time we spoke, it wasn't exactly what I would call a fun talk."

"Oh, nothing much. It's just a good day to have a good day!" he smiled.

"Okay, well, I guess that's the mood to be in! Now this will either make your day better or just stress you out! Do you want to come back to Granny's house with me for the last week I'm there?" I asked with a twinkle in my eye.

"Actually, that's not that difficult of a decision; I would love to see the old house again. So yeah, I'll come with you!"

"Oh, how exciting! Maybe you'll see Granny, Mum, and Dad!"

"You are not still going on after I told you that you were the one who killed them! They are dead! Way to ruin my good mood!"

"Look, I don't believe you, BUT let's go back to the house, and you can see for yourself."

"Yeah, whatever, I'm going to go and pack my things. I'll meet you back in here in around 20 minutes."

"Okay, that sounds good."

I then had to wait around for him to return, but at least I had tea with me and my little, big Chip. I am still very confused about what happened to him, but I still love him either way.

I sat waiting until he got back, which was around 30 minutes. Then we both got straight onto the train, and our journey back to Granny's house began. Not much happened other than a couple of drunk idiots having an argument, so I won't bore you with it, but we will start back outside the train station in my town.

We walked to the nearest bus stop but eventually realised that the next bus wasn't for an hour, and we weren't going to wait that long, so we just got a taxi. We probably could have just walked, but then we would have been really tired, and I just can't be bothered.

"Just the next left here, please," I said to the driver.

"No, right," he said, trying to correct me.

"No left! If we go right, then we will be going straight into a shop!" I exclaimed.

"I said right!" The driver shouted as he swerved down the street.

I had to lean forward and grab the wheel before we

smashed into the building ahead, but then I saw him. The antique store guy, Julian! He was our driver!

"Hey! What are you doing here?!" I questioned.

"If you won't listen to me, then I will force you to!" he shouted.

"Look, Julian, you can't do this!" Joe said.

Before I knew it, Julian had a knife in his hand and started slashing at me. No one was watching the wheel, and we smashed straight through his shop window, making me jolt forward. This doesn't sound that bad. Just a crash, but no... When I shot forward, the knife slashed through my stomach!

"Julian, what did you do?!" Joe screamed.

He got out of the car and ran up the street towards Granny's house. Why was he going there?

"Fo—ll—ow him, Joe," I stuttered in pain.

"No, we need to get you to the hospital!" he shouted in fear.

"Call me an am—bu—lance th—en g—o," I

stuttered.

"I can't just leave you here!" he said.

"Just go after him!" I shouted with the last of my strength.

After that, everything just kind of faded to black. Am I dead? It didn't feel like I was asleep, but it didn't feel like my life was over. I could still sort of hear things around me, like one guy saying "Room 17a" and someone else saying "Quick! Rush him to surgery!" So I think that I must be in some kind of hospital...

As there isn't much I can say when I'm pretty much dying on the spot, I'll give you around a page's worth of what I can hear around me.

"Pass me the needle," came a voice. I'm going to call voice 1.

"Okay, will you be needing a new set of gloves?" came another voice, which I'm going to call voice 2.

"Yes, please," answered voice 1.

"Do you think he will make it?" asked voice 2.

"To be honest with you, it's not looking likely," answered voice 1 in a doubtful tone.

"If he doesn't make it through, then that old house around the corner you always liked will probably be up for grabs," voice 2 said, making me feel angry.

"It's going up for auction in a week, you dimbo!" voice 1 said.

"Why do you hate me?" voice 2 asked.

"Look, I don't hate you, but I'm doing surgery, and you're talking to me about him dying!" voice 1 shouted.

After that, the room fell quiet for a while, and I didn't feel dead. I can only assume they finished the surgery, and I had to hope that it all went well.

About 2 hours passed

My vision suddenly started reappearing, completely blurry at first, then slowly coming back bit by bit. I had survived but awoke with no one by my side. Not my brother, not my family, no one...

I rang the buzzer next to me, which would call the doctors into my room, but the most embarrassing thing that could have happened, actually happened... When leaning over for the button, I rolled out of bed and crashed to the floor! OW! How it hurt so much!

Doctors came running in shouting for help, and I think I managed to rip the stitches they had only just put in. Already! I began shouting in pain and almost paddling in a pool of my own blood. I could feel myself passing out again, but I wouldn't let it happen! I have to fight and get out of this hospital. I need to make sure Joe is okay and find out if Julian has got him or the other way around.

"Sir, we need to get you up!" a doctor said to me in a panic.

"I ca- I can't move," I said, breathless.

"You are going to have to, sir; otherwise, you will bleed to death!" they shouted.

"Okay, okay, here I go!" I said in pain as I was lifted by doctors, making me feel like I was being stabbed a hundred times over in one spot.

Once I was back on the bed, I was put to sleep again for them to redo the stitches. Since I had only just woken up in the first place, this time I slept all the way through to the next day.

When I awoke, my brother sat by my side, and I felt happy in that moment. Still in pain, but happy.

"Morning sleepyhead!" Joe said to me with a smile.

"What happened to Julian?" I asked before anything else.

"I didn't see where he went... I saw him run into Granny's house, then I got a call from the hospital, so I came here and didn't see him again," he told me.

"Why didn't you follow him?" I complained.

"Because I was told you were going to die!" he

shouted.

"Well, if I was going to die anyway, then why didn't you just follow Julian?!"

"Sometimes you are really difficult. You know that!"

During this conversation, a doctor walked in to ask me a few questions about how I was feeling.

"Hey, so how are you doing now?" she asked.

"Just listen to him! Clearly, he's doing better; back to thinking he's indestructible," Joe said.

"Can you not?" I asked angrily.

"Yeah… yeah… Just get on with it," Joe said.

"Do you need a minute?" the doctor asked.

"No, it's fine. Let's get on with it, please," I asked.

"Okay… Well then, how are you feeling now?" she asked.

"I'm feeling a lot better but still in quite a bit of pain," I answered.

I got asked a bunch more questions about how I

was feeling and was told how the police would be in to ask some questions about who stabbed me. Well, that will be interesting, won't it? The day I get to put old man Julian in jail will be a good day for everyone! Well, it would be a good day if he wasn't the next person to walk through my hospital door!

"Julian, what do you think you're doing here?!" I shouted.

"Okay, you may think I'm crazy for stabbing you and all," he said.

"Crazy!? You're beyond crazy!" I screamed.

"DON'T INTERRUPT ME!" he shouted, "Like I was saying! You may think I'm crazy for stabbing you."

"Can someone get him out?! Why are we even listening to him?!" Joe shouted.

"Just let me finish!" he yelled.

"No, but why should we? The police will be here soon, and you will pay for what you've done! I don't want to hear anything you have to say!" I shouted.

"To be honest, I expected this from you, so I'm just going to say it! The mirror is what lets you see your parents! I stabbed you so that I could finally explain to you, without you running away, what the mirror can do," Julian shouted confidently.

"Mirror?" Joe questioned, "You stabbed him to talk about a mirror?!"

"Yeah, he doesn't stop going on about that stupid mirror," I grunted.

"Look. It's another world of its own. The opposite of our world, with a twist of older times! So yes, your parents are alive, but they shouldn't be! Your grandmother isn't meant to be there, and she is causing all kinds of problems!" he shouted, like he actually believed what he was saying.

Joe clicked the emergency call button, which made doctors come running over. I won't get into the details, but Julian was escorted out of the building, and I can only hope to the nearest jail.

"What was all that about?" I asked rhetorically.

"You didn't tell me anything about a mirror?" Joe asked.

We both began to laugh. Another world? Yeah right.

"He's talking about an old mirror in Granny's house that he claims to have made. It really is an amazing mirror, but I'm pretty sure it's not another world," I said.

"Maybe I could go check it out. I did want to see inside the old house," he said.

"Well, I want to come with you, but I don't know when I will be let out of this place," I said.

"Who knows… could be days, weeks, maybe even months," Joe joked.

"That's not even funny," I frowned.

"Okay… okay. I'll go and have a talk with the doctor," he said.

Joe went to talk to the doctors and nurses for me to find out when I would be freed, but in that time, I had already gotten changed and ready, as I wasn't just going to sit around all day!

"Okay, I spoke to them, and they don't think you are ready yet, but it really does depend on how you feel," he stated, "It's not something they would usually do, but they need the space urgently, and well, a little money helped the situation."

"You bribed them to let me go early!?" I questioned. "Joe, I can't ask you to do that!"

"It's fine… and also already done. So I hope you're feeling ready?" he asked.

"I'm not feeling great as I was stabbed yesterday, but yes, I still want to leave!" I stated.

"Okay, well, we've got to go and pick up Chip, then I guess we can head straight home," he said.

"Wait… Where is Chip!?!?!?" I freaked out.

"Don't worry, I got a dog sitter for him. Luckily, it

wasn't that difficult to find one in a hurry."

"Oh, okay, that makes me feel a bit better."

The doctors entered the room rather quietly. I suppose the bribe had something to do with that. They followed the protocol and asked me how I was feeling and if I was up to leaving, and of course they already knew the answer. Then they brought a wheelchair in and left me to leave with Joe.

NOT BY TAXI THIS TIME!!!

But instead, we walked, and by we, I mean my brother walked, and he pushed me along in my wheelchair. It didn't take long to get back as the hospital wasn't that far from the house; nothing was very far from the house as it was pretty much in the centre of everything.

"Wow, the old house," Joe said with a tear rolling down his cheek.

"Yep, in all its glory," I said.

"Is that a note on the door?" Joe questioned.

"Yes, it's probably from Julian," I said with a sigh, until I read it.

. . . .

To Mr Lucus Widdley,

I am contacting you to let you know we have not been able to access the property, meaning we have been unable to complete your construction.

We understand you already have our number, and if we don't hear from you in the next few days, then we will have to take extreme precautions.

From The Construction Company.

. . . .

Oh… I may have forgotten about them. Oh well, I wasn't gone for long. I will just contact them later.

"Not to worry, just the builders I have doing some work on the house," I told my brother.

"Ah, okay…" he replied.

We walked/wheeled in through the doors, and Joe had the same reaction as me! His jaw dropped to the ground, as even your memory can't remember the beauty of this house. I mean, even I was still amazed by it.

I gave him a quick tour around, and by quick, I mean it took about an hour due to the 12 bedrooms there are, and the house is just massive in general. The last room we arrived at was Granny's' room—yep, that's right, the one with the mirror. The all-powerful mirror...

"So, the last and final room is Granny's room. And that over there is the mirror," I pointed out to Joe.

"Ah, the all-powerful mirror is it," Joe sniggered.

He walked over and took a look around it while I quickly popped to the bathroom, but when I came back, I couldn't find him. He wasn't at the mirror anymore, and I couldn't hear him anywhere in the house.

"Joe! Joe! Hello!" I shouted.

No reply

"Okay, very funny. Where are you?" I shouted again.

Still no reply.

I wheeled myself into the bedroom and over to the mirror, as I thought maybe he may be hiding behind it as a joke. I looked all around but still couldn't see him. How could he disappear in the same time it took me to go to the toilet?

Suddenly, I heard him! He was downstairs. Maybe Mum and Dad are home!

"Joe, are you down there?" I shouted.

"Ye- ye- yes," he stuttered.

I had to leave my wheelchair and hobble down the stairs, as this time I didn't have Joe to help me. There, I saw him. Talking to Mum and Dad. It did make me realise I haven't had a proper conversation with my dad yet. But finally, Joe would believe me!

"See, I wasn't lying!" I stated.

"Hey, who is this you have brought into our house?" my mum shouted.

"What do you mean, Mum? It's me…" Joe said.

"You! I don't know who you are!" she exclaimed.

"Joe! They had some memory loss or something. They don't remember us," I sighed.

"And you couldn't have told me about that beforehand?" he questioned.

"Memory loss! Look, I could just about tolerate you," she said to me, "but there is another person who thinks they are my child. This is getting a bit ridiculous now!"

"Lucas, what is going on?" Joe shouted.

"I'm going to call the police," Dad said.

"Why do you always go straight to calling the police!?" I questioned.

"Look, I've just found out that somehow my parents are alive even though I watched you kill them, and now we are talking about calling the police and memory loss!" Joe screeched.

"What do you mean he killed us?!" Mum and Dad shouted.

"What is all the noise out here?" Granny asked as she came out of the dining room.

"Granny!" Joe shouted in joy.

"Don't worry, Mum, I'm going to call the police," Mum said to Granny.

"Oh, that won't be necessary. Let me talk to them," Granny persuaded our parents.

Granny grabbed the sleeves of our t-shirts and walked us to the dining room out of the way of our parents, then she pulled us both together and gave us the biggest hug ever.

"I've missed you both so much!" she whimpered.

"So, you remember?" Joe asked.

"Granny, what happened the last time I saw you?" I asked.

"Where have you been all this time!?" Joe questioned.

"Why did you lock me in a bedroom?" I asked.

"Okay... Okay... I get the point. Come and sit down, and I'll answer all your questions," she answered.

We walked over to the dining table, and we all sat around it. Finally, I'm going to get some answers!

"First, before I answer your questions, I need to ask you one of my own first... Have you met Julian? The town antique guy?" she asked, leaving me pale white.

"Um, yes, we have," I answered.

"I don't know how to tell you this, but I'm married to the man," she said.

"Your what?!" Joe and I shouted at the same time.

"I had a feeling you would have met him as he comes to visit me sometimes... But yes, it's true. I married him a few years ago; well, that is through all the other worlds and all... very complicated," she said.

"What?! You mean he was telling the truth about everything?" I shouted in astonishment.

"I don't believe you!" Joe shouted before storming out of the room.

"Lucas, you need to go get him! There's a lot of things that can go wrong with him being out there!" she warned me.

"What do you mean? What could go wrong?" I questioned.

"There's no time to explain! You need to go get him!" she shouted.

"But wait a minute! I have just been stabbed by your husband!" I explained.

"He did what? Oh well, look at your wound now anyway," she said.

I lifted my shirt and couldn't believe my eyes. I was astonished. "I'm healed!? But how?"

"Like I said, go get your brother, then I will explain!" she exclaimed.

I got out of my seat and left to look for Joe. I couldn't believe everything that was going on right now! I mean, is all this real? Am I going insane? Everything was just moving all too fast! I don't know what to believe anymore. Either way, I need to find Joe; he couldn't have left more than 2 minutes ago. I should be able to catch him if I hurry.

Luckily, he hadn't gone far at all; he was sitting on a bench just across the street from the house but was looking more disappointed than anything else.

I walked over to him and asked, "Hey. Are you okay?"

"Well... I just don't really know what to say anymore," he answered.

"I understand... I get how emotional you must be feeling. Confused, happy, sad, and just straight-up mad! Trust me, I've been through it! I know all you need is time and space, but right now, Granny needs us inside. She seemed pretty insistent on it," I sighed.

"See, even though that sentence doesn't make sense, they were meant to be dead... How are they walking and talking right now?!" he questioned.

"Look... I did tell you."

"Really?! You're going with I told you so after I've just found out my parents aren't dead after you killed them?"

"Um... yes..."

"You are unbelievable. You really are."

"You didn't believe me?! Why should I have to be there for you!?"

He got up off the bench and laughed. He stormed back to the house like I had said he needed to, which was lucky as I really wasn't in the mood to chase him around the town at the moment.

When we were walking up to the house, we noticed Granny sitting on the front step, waiting for us.

"It's so weird seeing her there," Joe whispered into my ear.

I laughed a bit.

"Quick, get inside, you two! You can't be out here for long," Granny hurried us in.

"Why, what's the rush?" I asked.

"I'll explain inside. Just hurry in now!" she rushed.

We quickly ran into the house, feeling like we were being chased by something. We were moving so quickly.

"Okay stop! What is the big deal!?" I asked.

"Look, there's no time to explain... You need to leave before everything falls apart!" she screeched.

"You just rushed us in. Now you want us to leave?" Joe questioned.

"Yeah, what's going on?" I asked.

"No, I don't want you out of the house; I want you out of this world!" she stated.

"Well, that makes more sense," I said sarcastically.

"Duh, we should have known," Joe laughed.

"If I'm going to be honest, I still don't necessarily

believe in this whole-world stuff," I announced.

"Oh, for goodness' sake, just come with me!" she said.

We followed her upstairs and over to the mirror.

"Simple as that," she said, standing in the door frame.

"Simple as what?" Joe asked.

"Just look into the mirror," she said.

"Wait, where's Lucas?!" Joe shouted as he turned to the mirror, but when he turned back around, "Lucas? How did you just appear there?!"

"More like, how did you and Granny just disappear?!" I shouted.

"Where's Granny gone?!" Joe asked.

"Wait, so it really is another world?" I finally began to believe what Julian had been telling us.

"Woah, this is so cool!" Joe shouted in excitement.

"Wait. But doesn't that mean my stab wound should be back? Why's it still gone? Not that I'm complaining," I said.

"I don't really know, but just enjoy it, I guess."

"I suppose… But what did Granny mean about the world falling apart? I'm going to say something I know I'm going to regret. But we need to talk to Julian."

"Well, as much as I hate to admit it, I think you're right."

"I can't believe he's married to Granny, that there's another world, that our parents are alive, and…"

"Okay. Stop. You are sounding crazy now!"

"Oh sorry… just a bit excited."

We then had to go and meet Julian, obviously, but first I wouldn't let us go and meet him without picking up my little Chipster from his dog sitter.

I didn't realise when Joe had told me that Chip was with a dog sitter; he actually just meant he had left him with some random person on the streets claiming to be a dog sitter. I mean, how stupid can you really be?

Luckily, he still had an address that he was given, yet we don't actually know if it's a real address. But you've really got to hope for the best in these situations.

We hurried as quickly as we could, which wasn't very fast, but I needed to make sure he was okay.

When we finally arrived, which felt like it took forever, we had gotten really lucky to not have been robbed. Chip was there and back with me, but for the bill, they charged!

"So, payment will be £780.89," the dog sitter said with a grin.

"I'm sorry, how much?!" I gasped.

"Well, it was a late booking; what do you expect?" they shouted.

"Not an almost £800 bill, that's for sure! I will not be paying that much!" I screeched.

"Well, you can't just not pay me," they said while

muttering something under their breath.

I threw a £20 bill at them and walked away with Joe. I'm not paying that ridiculous amount of money for someone to look after my dog for not even a whole day!

I could hear them shouting behind us that they were going to call the police on us, and blah blah blah. But, I mean, we are on the way to the police station anyway.

"Joe. Do you want a weird thought?" I asked randomly.

"Um… That depends on what it is," he replied in a nervous voice.

"Our family is all dead in this world… No one else will know that they are alive, and technically, we are still orphans."

"That is quite a weird thought."

"What if we never went back?"

"Why would we ever do that!? Are you losing your

mind?!"

"Well, if Granny comes back, then technically the house is hers, and I mean, you won't be able to just keep all that money... whereas if we destroy the mirror and everything/everyone inside, then we can keep it all."

"Look! I don't care what you do, but I am going to go back and see them as soon as I can! How could you even care about the money!?"

"You're right, sorry... I don't even know what I was thinking."

"Look, I know there's a lot going on, so I'll let you off, but you have to promise me that you won't leave them!"

"No, I won't. I'm sorry that I even thought that."

We couldn't keep walking everywhere, as it was getting rather tiring, so we decided to go and rent a car for the last few days I had the house. Yes, I'm still selling the house. No, Joe doesn't know. I will still be taking the mirror with me, but my plans for the mirror are different from Joe's. But I'll get into that later.

It didn't take us too long to get to the police station once we had the car, but a part of me just wanted to turn back and go home; he only stabbed me two days ago.

"Are we sure we want to talk to him?" I asked.

"We kind of have to if we want to find out about the mirror and the other world. I really need to stop saying that. It makes me sound insane," he answered.

"Maybe if I just wait in the car with Chip," I said.

"You can if you really want to, but then you might miss out on everything that he tells me... You know my memory is awful; I'll probably forget everything," he said, getting out of the car.

"No, I really should talk to him," I said anxiously.

"Okay, do you want to come or not?!" he asked.

"Yes, okay, I'll come," I decided.

I got out of the car with Joe and brought Chip out

with me too (It's a book. I can bring a dog wherever I want.).

As we walked in, everyone turned and stared at us with the glare of a thousand needles.

"Um, Lucas, look at this," Joe pointed to a poster with our faces on it. Apparently, we are being looked for about a theft of a home... Granny's home! My home! The house…

"RUN!" I shouted.

With Chip in my arms and a mind full of confusion, we charged as fast as we could, trying to make it back to the car. I could just about touch the handle before an officer jumped me and threw me to the ground. Joe managed to get away.

"Hey! What are you doing?! I haven't done anything wrong!" I shouted.

"Don't act stupid! You know exactly what you have done! Now that's enough chitchat from you!" the officer stated.

"Let go of me!" I said, trying to wriggle my way out of handcuffs.

Once again, I am being dragged off to a cell, and once again, for reasons I will never know. I never stole a thing!

Chip had run off somewhere when I was pushed to the ground, and I just hope for his sake that Joe finds him, as otherwise, I don't know where he could be. It would kill me to lose him; it seemed he was the only one I could talk to when no one would believe me about my family.

I was taken straight into the witness room and questioned about things I didn't have a clue about.

"Okay. So, let's cut to the point. Were you in the Walker's family home between 2 pm and 4 pm today?" one officer asked.

"To be honest with you, I don't know who the Walker's family is," I said confused.

"Okay... Well, if you don't know the family, you

were just robbing a random house. Is that what you're saying?" the other officer asked me.

"Let me rephrase my question. Were you in the biggest house that is in our town between 2 pm and 4 pm today!?" the first officer questioned.

"Well obviously… I do-" I started to say before I was interrupted.

"So, you admit to breaking into the house," the first officer smirked.

"No, I li-" I was once again interrupted.

"On this date of July 17th, 2022, at 12:25 pm, Mr Lucas Widdley has been arrested for theft of the Walkers family home," the officer said into the camera.

"Wait but…" I started saying.

"You have the right to remain silent, and anything you say or do will be held against you in a court of law," the officer said, walking me off to a cell.

I didn't say much more on the way to the cell

because they wouldn't let me finish a sentence, but when we got there, I met my roommate.

"JULIAN! No officers, I cannot be in this cell!" I shouted. Even though I wanted to talk to him, I would rather not be stuck in a cell with him!

I understand that usually you wouldn't be placed with the person who stabbed you, but this must have something to do with the whole world's merging... Great...

"Oh, I'm sorry, did you want the first-class cell!?" they said sarcastically.

I stopped talking and just let what was happening happen. Once the officers had left me in the cell with Julian, I took advantage of this hell to ask him some questions.

"Well, you got your way, didn't you?" Julian hissed.

"Um, what do you mean?" I questioned.

"Just look at me. I am in jail! Thanks to you!" he

shouted.

"YOU STABBED ME!" I screamed a bit too loud. Luckily, no one heard.

"Yes and? It was only so I could tell you about the mirror. Which didn't even work anyway! You still wouldn't listen to me!" he shouted back.

"Actually, I did... We went through the mirror. I believe you now," I stated.

"Oh, really, so you're telling me I'm not lying!" he said sarcastically.

"I know I should have believed you, but you were trying to get me to believe in another world... You can't expect anyone to believe that easily. Then you stabbed me! I thought you were just insane."

"Whatever. You have just ruined my life; you made me lose my store and my wife."

"How did you lose your store? It will still be there once you get out, won't it?"

"Okay, maybe I'm being a bit dramatic... But you

still ruined my life!"

"Yeah, we found out about you and Granny, and we didn't mean to separate you two, but why didn't you just tell me?" I asked.

"Oh, because you would have believed that, would you?" he replied.

"I suppose not."

"How much else do you know about the other world?"

"Not much, but Granny did keep on rushing us to leave, saying that we were making things fall apart."

"Are things really getting that bad over there?"

"What do you mean?"

"It's quite a lot to explain. How much time have you got?" Julian asked.

"How much time do you think?! Were in a prison cell!"

"Okay. No need to be sarcastic."

"Are we really having this conversation right

now!?”

"Okay, back to the mirror.”

“Please!” I shouted.

"Actually, no," he said with a frown on his face.

“No?” I questioned.

“No. I will not tell you anything more about the mirror. You took everything I have, so now I refuse to help you.”

“Really? You know what? I don’t care about it. Once I’m out of this place, I’ll just go back and ask Granny everything.”

“Yeah, once you’re out of here..." he muttered.

“What was that?!”

“Nothing!”

We sat in silence for the rest of the night. Boring!

When I awoke, I expected it to be around early sunrise, but no, it was 2 am, and some people were screaming in the cell opposite, awakening me. You don't know how much I wanted to or needed to leave this place.

I have to hope that Joe finds a way to get me out of here, legal or not!

4 and a half hours later

It was impossible for me to fall back to sleep as I stayed up worrying about everything and listening to screaming inmates. But I was soon greeted by a police officer waking everyone up.

Here is my prison schedule:

06:30 Wake-up

06:30 – 06:45 Morning exercises, personal hygiene, and making the beds

06:45 – 07:15 Free time for prisoners who are not engaged in work during that period

07:15 – 07:45 Breakfast

07:45 – 08:00 free time for prisoners who are not engaged in work during that period

08:00 – 08:30 Morning roll-call

08:30 – 12:30 Free time for prisoners who are not engaged in work or studies during that period

12:30 – 13:00 Lunch

13:00 – 17:00 Free time for prisoners who are not engaged in work or studies during that period

17:00 – 17:30 Dinner

17:30 – 20:00 Free time for prisoners who are not engaged in work during that period

20:00 – 20:30 Evening roll-call

20:30 – 06:30 Sleep Time.

And that is my schedule.

<u>*6:30 am — Exercise*</u>

So, I got up and made my bed, brushed my teeth with toothpaste that tasted like chalk, and went out for my exercise, which was painful so early in the morning.

But not all was so bad... Although that is how it seemed.

While I was out on the exercise field, I saw something on the other side of the fence, which surprised me; it was Joe pretending his car had broken down. Well, I think he was pretending. I don't know what his plan was, but I really wanted to keep watching and find out. Although as hard as I tried to keep my eyes on him, I kept getting shouted at by the guards for not exercising. I took one more quick look to see what he was doing, yet he was gone in less than a minute!

He was probably grabbed by some officers or something and arrested. But who knows?

I continued working out for the small amount of 15 minutes we had before moving on to the next subject, which was free time! But for only 30 minutes, I need to use my time wisely. But there wasn't really much to do...

Wait! I saw Joe's car (the rental car) driving away from the prison! What was he doing? He knows there's police looking for him. I don't know how he hasn't been seen already.

6:45 am — Free time

Now, with absolutely nothing to do and no reason to do anything, I sat on a bench and stared at the roads beyond. You see, this prison is built far out of any town, so there are just roads going on for miles.

Eventually, after about 10 minutes of sitting on the bench, Julian came and sat next to me, which I was rather surprised about. He only told me he wanted nothing to do with me last night.

"So, I know we didn't exactly agree last night," he said.

"Yeah, you can say that again," I snickered.

"Like I was saying, I know we didn't exactly agree last night, but you've got to know I can't tell you everything," he said.

"Why though? Why can't you tell me everything?" I asked.

"Because it's too much for your little mind to comprehend!" he replied.

"HEY!" I shouted. "You know what? That's fine. Joe will be here to get me out soon anyway," I stated.

"What why? How do you know?"

"Well, I don't know... But I saw him outside the prison earlier, so I can only assume he's doing something."

"Aren't the police looking for him?"

"Yeah, they are, and I did wonder why he was so close earlier and not being chased after, but yeah, I actually don't know."

"Oh no… Did you see anyone else notice him?"

"Well, actually, now you mention it... I don't think I did, but I wasn't really paying attention."

"Oh no… no… no… no… It can't all be happening this quick!"

"What?! What's happening?!"

"Okay, I think I'm really going to have to hope we can get out of here soon, as if we don't, this could be terrible for everyone."

"Just get to the point!"

The bell rang, calling everyone in for breakfast right before Julian was about to finally tell me what was going on.

7:15 am — Breakfast

Julian and I sat across from each other in the cafeteria but ate in silence, so all the other prisoners crowded around us couldn't hear everything about the mirror.

I ate a lovely meal for breakfast! It was surprisingly nice for prison food, which is what I would say if it wasn't just a pile of mush on a tray.

There's not much more to say about breakfast, but for the rest of it, I mainly just sat still and waited till the next part of the day.

7:45 am — Free time... again

Once more, I was back outside, sitting on the bench with Julian. Where we could finally finish our conversation.

"Okay, finally, I can finish what I was going to say. Basically, with people from our world being in the other world, it will slowly start falling apart and merging with this world," he nervously announced.

"But doesn't that mean that our parents will be alive in this world?" I said.

"Well, no, not exactly... It will kill them. And with

Patricia (Granny) being there, she will also die, but die in the sense that she never existed."

"WHAT?!??! But if she never existed, then..."

"Yes, you would also have never existed."

"But how's Granny been there all this time?!"

"Well, she hasn't been going in and out of the mirror continuously; besides, she is only one person," he said.

Okay, I sort of understand why he wouldn't tell me now. I really needed to get out of this place to warn Joe!

"Look, I need to get out of here! You're an old, antique kind of guy; have you read anything about people escaping from here before?"

"I have, but only things from the past that have now been fixed up and are definitely not usable anymore."

"Okay, well, that's not very helpful."

For the rest of our free time, we just sat again, this

time with a sense of fear throughout. I am locked away and could disappear at any moment without any control whatsoever. I can only assume my brother is trying to help me escape from the other world, but just his being there is killing both of us.

8:00 am — Morning roll-call

We all gathered around when the guards called us for the morning roll call.

Roll-call: A way to count and make sure everyone is around

8:30 am — Free time AGAIN

I wasn't going to sit around this time waiting for something to happen, but instead, I decided to sneak around the prison a little bit to try and find a way to escape. It's very unlikely that I will find a way, but you never know...

Being sneaky was key to this plan; there were guards at every corner, cameras at every angle, and people ready to snitch at every turn! Also, running with about an hour of sleep didn't help. I didn't really know where to start.

Possibly, if I tried befriending a guard, that might work. Although if another inmate finds out, I'll be at the top of their beat-up list for sucking up to a guard.

I'm sure it'll be fine.

I went out to the courtyard area, where there was an officer standing at the entrance. My plan was to make up some random excuse, like, If you help me escape, I'll tell you where your missing mother is. Then just hope for the best that he has a missing mother. I mean, if that doesn't work, then I'm sure that nothing much will happen. I hope…

"Hey, Mr Officer Guy," I said awkwardly.

"Don't talk to me," he said.

"Well, I just have a small question," I said.

"Not interested!" he stated.

"Well, you will be interested!" I said into his ear in a threatening tone. "If you help me get out of this hell,

I will get you your mother back!"

"My mama?" he sobbed.

Shockingly, it seems he did have a missing mum. What a coincidence!

Unless he's faking it, that would be unlikely, though. I think…

"I know where she is, and I can get her back for you, but you have to get me out of here!" I exclaimed.

"Okay. I'll help you, but you need a key that Officer Smith has," he told me.

"And how am I supposed to get that?"

"During lunch, he stands waiting in the doorway of the courtyard area to make sure people aren't trying to leave when they aren't supposed to. Your job is to find a way to knock him out or somehow take the key."

"Okay, well, what if you just distract him and I take the key out of his pocket?"

"Are you an idiot?! I shouldn't leave my post! And

besides, we aren't exactly on the best of terms... Then there's also the fact that he doesn't just keep the key to leave the prison in his pocket."

"You've got to be kidding me!"

"Look, you've just got to discretely knock him out, then snatch the key!"

He walked away towards the cafeteria, as lunch was next.

12:30 pm — Lunch

Once again, I sat in the cafeteria, eating the slop that we were fed. My heart was racing, as what I was about to do next could get me locked up for life. Although that could be safer at this point.

I stood from my chair, alerting all the surrounding prisoners. How dare I stand during lunch?! Am I asking for more food?! No one ever does that. Imagine if I turned around and shouted, Sorry, just about to knock out a guard... There is no need to be alerted.

As I walked over towards Officer Smith standing

by the door, all the eyes that rested upon me returned to their slop.

Now to put a very quickly thought-out plan into action...

My Plan:

Step 1: Ask to be taken to the cell toilets, as you have to be accompanied during lunch hours.

Step 2: While walking towards the cell, I will look for a place with no officers nearby (which would be difficult).

Step 3: Once in the clear, I will trip him over and steal his taser.

Step 4: I will then taser him and take the key to the front gates, where the officer should be waiting for me.

Now to put my plan into action...

Instantly, Officer Smith stood out in front of me, ensuring I went no further.

"Hello," I said. "Could I go to the toilet?"

"Ufff," he huffed, "fine, follow me."

I followed him down the hall, waiting for my chance to act, but everywhere I looked, there were police officers.

Around all the corners of every tiny space, there was another officer. It was insane! How am I meant to carry out my plan?!

All was about to change...

As we were walking, he suddenly froze still, and I don't know if it was the prison slop doing something to my mind, but he slowly started burning away, crumbling into ash! And he wasn't the only one. As I looked around, everyone started disintegrating!

"RUN!" Julian shouted from behind me.

"What's going on?!" I shouted back.

"Just go!" he screeched.

Okay... I don't need to hear any more; I just need to hurry up and get out! That was until I stopped, but not because I was disappearing, but because of what I saw outside the prison windows/bars. Joe was driving around outside with the mirror attached to the front of the car. He was sending all the officers through!

That must be why people were beginning to disappear! The worlds are merging, meaning some people don't exist in the other world, some people don't exist in this world, and soon they won't exist in either! And Joe is slowly destroying all of existence!

"JOE, STOP!" I tried shouting out the window/bars.

I hurried down the stairs and through the hallways, easier than ever due to the prison literally changing all around me, becoming how it once was when it was first built.

"Joe, Stop!" I shouted again, now outside. "You're going to kill us all!"

He pulled up in the rental car next to me and signalled for me to jump in.

"No, you need to stop, Joe! The more people from

this world you send through will destroy that world and this world!" I yelled.

The car he was sitting in suddenly vanished too, making him and the mirror fall to the ground.

"NO!" I screamed as I ran over to the mirror.

"Ah, thanks for the help," Joe said, standing up from the ground.

"NO! This is serious, Joe! You cracked the mirror!" I cried.

The mirror lay on the ground with a crack from one corner to the other and seemed to be continuously growing, more at a slow pace but definitely growing.

"Where's Julian?" Joe asked, "Did you manage to talk to him? Maybe he would know how to fix this."

"Um… Yes… I did, but I don't know if he made it out of the building," I stated.

"Get it together, Lucas! You grab one corner of the mirror, and I'll grab the other!" Joe said enthusiastically. "We'll take it back to the house and try to talk to Granny!”

“You realise, Joe. If we go into the mirror, we could very well end up destroying the world," I stated.

“You don't know until you try," he grinned.

“I suppose that's the right attitude. Sort of…"

"Hey, what do you think happens if all the worlds merge? Do you think we would live?”

“I don't know much about it all still, but I'm pretty sure it's random who stays and goes, so I would say we have a 50/50 chance."

"Ah, well, that puts my mind at rest, I guess."

We continued on with the mirror for about half a mile before a young couple in a car pulled over and asked us if we needed a lift. The car was magnificent; it was one of those expensive old-school roof-off kinds of cars.

“Hey, you two look like you could use a hand with that," the woman offered.

“Why don't you hop into the back there, and we'll

give you a ride?" the man offered in a friendly tone.

"I think we're okay, but thank you," I said not wanting to get into a car with random strangers from a different time zone.

"No, don't be silly! Sorry, my brother here seems to only care about what he wants," Joe said. "We would happily accept a ride from you, as long as it's not a bother."

"No bother at all; hop right in!" they said excitedly.

"Joe, what are you doing!?" I whispered into his ear.

"Getting us home before the world ends!" he said.

"You realise these people seem to be a part of the world merging!" I said.

"How could you know that?" he asked.

"Because the newspaper on their back seats dates to the year 1987," I stated.

"You could have pointed that out before!" he said.

"Whatever we have to go now," I said in an

annoyed tone.

"Or maybe not," Joe said with a smirk.

"What does that mean?" I sighed.

Joe lifted the mirror up, facing the kind couple in the car. Yes, they were gone.

"Why would you do that?!" I shouted.

"Well, if it's destroying the world with everything merging, then what if we sent everything and everyone back!?" he said, as if he had just saved the world.

"The world is merging into one," I said.

"Yes and..."

"Listen again. The WORLD is merging into one."

"Okay, I get your point, but we have got to do something!"

"Well, for now, we have a stolen car, so I'm going to use that to my advantage and drive home."

We got into the car and continued on towards the house with a lot less struggle than it was carrying the mirror, but it still wasn't the best thing to steal the car.

How did he even get the mirror off the wall in the first place?

"Joe, I actually have a question for you," I said. "Were you outside the prison this morning, but in the other world?"

"Yeah, I got the worlds mixed up, but how do you know that?" he asked.

"I saw you."

"That's kind of embarrassing."

"Well, I mean, to be honest, that should be the least of your worries considering everything that is happening."

We eventually pulled up in the driveway of the house, where we didn't bother hanging the mirror back in Granny's' room but just leaned it up against a wall in the hallway so we could hurry up and go through to the other side.

Once we had put it down, you could tell the crack

had grown larger, and yes, we were looking straight at the mirror, expecting to be in the other world with Granny. But no, it wasn't working! The mirror wasn't letting us through!

"What's going on, Joe?!" I panicked.

"I don't know... Why should I know!? I don't know anything?!" he said almost too quickly.

"Joe... What aren't you telling me?" I questioned.

"I'm not telling you. I'm not, not telling you anything," he said.

"We may not have seen each other in years, but I can tell when you're lying to me."

"Okay... Granny told me some stuff while you were locked away," he said. "She told me that we have to make a decision. We have to pick a world to destroy, as both cannot live with one another peacefully."

"Well, that's easy. We just bring our family to this world and then destroy that world," I said.

"You've got to think about all the other lives in that world! Even though to us it's just another place that was created by Julian, to them it's a life with happiness and sadness, with family and pets. Not just something we can destroy without causing suffering."

"So we destroy our world, then?"

"Exactly!"

"Okay, cool, I'm good with that. NOT!" I exclaimed. "There's no difference which world we destroy! Both are full of lives!"

"Well, then what do you want to do?! I'm not made of answers!?!?!? I'm sick of you thinking that I know everything! Figure it out yourself for once!"

"Figure it out myself for once?! Says the person who wouldn't even believe me in the first place!"

"Okay! Children, calm yourself!" Julian exclaimed as he emerged from behind us.

"Where did you come from?" I Jumped.

"Well, after you abandoned me at the prison, I had

to get out myself, which wasn't that easy with everything changing and moving around!" he answered.

"I didn't abandon you! You told me to run!" I shouted.

"Yes, but usually people still try to help if they can!" he stated.

"Sounds like my selfish brother," Joe snarked.

"Oh, will you shut up?!" I said.

"Will you both shut up?!" Julian shouted. "We need to get this mirror fixed so we can save the world!"

"You can fix it?" I asked.

"Obviously. I didn't create something that not even I could fix," he said.

"So how do we fix it then?" Joe asked.

"I'm getting to that," Julian said. "We need a sacrifice to begin with."

"A SACRIFICE!" Joe and I gasped.

"No, obviously not! I'm just joking with you. But we do need the blood of the most powerful person in this room, and I hate to say it, but that is you, Lucas," Julian said.

"Me? How am I powerful in any way?!" I asked.

"You are the child of powerful magic. You weren't born like most but instead created," Julian announced.

"I'm sorry, what? So, mum and dad, aren't mum and dad?" I questioned.

"Oh, so you're not my brother..." Joe said.

"I created you. The mirror was created for you. The world inside is your own. When I created the mirror, you were a child taken from inside. A magical child. My child," Julian sobbed.

"So, you're my dad. I'm not real," I said in disbelief.

"You are as real as can be, and don't ever doubt that!" he shouted.

"So, if you're not even my brother, then why did you kill my parents!?" Joe shouted.

"I didn't!" I shouted back, not wanting to believe it.

"Actually, you kind of did and didn't," Julian said.

"What's that supposed to mean?" I asked.

"Yeah!? I watched him kill them," Joe stated.

"Okay… Basically, it was Joe who killed your parents," Julian said.

"What me?! How could I have done it when it was me who watched Lucas do it?" Joe shouted.

"You WATCHED me do it? You're saying you saw me get a knife and stab my parents in their sleep when I was just a young boy!" I screeched.

"Well, no… Um, well, yes, I guess," Joe stuttered.

"WHAT KIND OF PSYCHOPATH LETS THEIR YOUNGER BROTHER MURDER THEIR PARENTS!?" I bellowed.

"WAIT!" Julian shouted. "Before you kill each

other, you should let me finish."

"Okay, well, you better hurry before I commit another murder!" I threatened.

"Well, that's just the thing. You haven't committed a murder. Joe did it," Julian stated.

"What are you talking about? I watched him!?" Joe said.

"Yeah, even I'm a bit confused now," I said.

"Joe killed your parents the same way you thought Lucas had; however, once he had done so, he managed to convince Lucas that it was his fault at such a young age... And Joe grew into his own lie." Julian revealed.

"What..." I muttered.

"Patricia (Granny) had then carried out the lie to relieve Lucas of the pain, making him think it was her. But she was taken away not long after," Julian announced.

"But why... why would Joe do that?" I asked.

"Look, the world is ending. I could get into everything that has happened in the past, or we could just sort out getting to tomorrow and then talk about this after that," Julian stated.

I wanted to know why. I wanted answers. But I understood that saving the world was probably more important.

"Who are you in my house?!" a woman walked into the hallway and asked.

"Who are you?!" I shouted back.

"This is my house!" she said. "Hey, I think I recognise you from somewhere?!"

"No, this is my house!" I shouted.

"I just bought this house! I know where I recognise you from. You stole my dog!" she screeched.

"I forgot to tell you that if the other world is locked and the worlds are merging, it can start creating new things, like someone else owning this house," Julian told us.

"Huh?" Joe sighed.

"Chip? He's my dog?! I didn't steal any dogs! Wait, where is Chip?!" I shouted.

"Yes, Chip! He's my dog!" the woman exclaimed.

If this woman did exist outside of the merging worlds, then she could very well be Chip's real family.

"I found Chip," I stuttered.

"You stole him from us!" she yelled. "I was told the filthy scum who stole my dog was in jail!"

"Okay, I think we should leave and get the stuff together for repairing the mirror," Julian hurried.

"WAIT! Where is my dog?" I shouted.

"I have him! Don't think I'm letting you have him!" the woman yelled.

"Okay… Just tell me your name," I asked.

"Not that it's any of your business, but if it will get you out quicker, I will tell you... My name is Carlie," she said.

"Okay… Carlie. With the amount going on right

now, it's not safe for Chip to be with me. So as long as you promise he will have a loving home with a caring family, I will leave him with you," I said this with tears falling from my face into a puddle beneath me.

"Of course he will! He already does! You wouldn't even be allowed to take him away if you wanted to! He's MINE!" she shouted.

"Okay, goodbye, Chip," I sobbed as I walked out of the building.

Without Chip, every day wasn't going to be as good as it was with him, but as long as I know he's got a good life, then this is for the best.

"Okay, so we need my blood then..." I stuttered, trying to get my mind off of Chip.

"Yes, but that's not all we need for the mirror; that's just one of the things we need," Julian said.

"How are we supposed to easily get blood out without just slicing through Lucas?" Joe asked.

"Yeah? How do we not cut me open?" I questioned.

"We will take you to the hospital and get them to draw blood from you," Julian suggested.

"And you think the hospital is just going to let us in and take blood?" I asked.

"I don't even know if the hospital still stands?! IF and I mean, IF, the hospital is still there, then we will find another solution, but for now, that's our best bet!" Julian stated.

We got into our stolen car and headed towards the hospital, but at a slow pace due to looking around at all the old buildings, cars, and even people that had all slowly begun to change.

But we did eventually arrive at the hospital, which was shockingly smaller than before! But still, with people inside, this put our plan at a stopping point, but evidently, we couldn't just sit around with the world falling apart.

"So, what now?" I asked.

"I don't know..." Julian answered.

"You don't know!? That's a change?!" Joe said in a surprised tone.

"I think we should get some rest and then come up with a plan in the morning. How does that sound to everyone?" I asked.

"That would sound great if we had somewhere to stay," Julian said.

"Well, can't we stay at yours, Julian?" Joe asked.

"My apartment above the shop? Well, that would depend on if someone is living up there in the new merged world," Julian said.

"Only one way to find out," I said.

We got back into the stolen car and headed towards the antique store, which was in the opposite direction of the way we had originally come from, so it took a rather long time. We knew that the apartment would definitely be there, as Julian made sure of that when creating the world… my world… Which is weird to say, but yet we didn't quite know if someone else would be living there or not.

"If there is someone living there, then where do we go?" Joe asked from the backseat of the car.

"We could sleep in the park. I've slept there once," I mentioned.

Everyone just sat in silence the rest of the way, mainly wondering why I had slept in the park. I did have a thought of getting a hotel, but I didn't say anything because it would be hilarious if Joe and Julian had to sleep in a park!

<u>At the shop</u>

When the car pulled up outside of the shop, it was… you could say different to when I had first seen it; by different, I mean… a few less items, *empty*.

"Everything might be gone, but at least with everything merging, the front of the antique store had rebuilt itself after our little incident earlier," Joe said, trying to make things positive.

"True…" I said, "Still not quite over that, by the way."

Julian said nothing at this time, as I think he had just about had enough of us.

We went into a small closet-like room in the shop, which held a ladder inside leading up to the apartment building. Yes, a ladder.

"Well, at least we have somewhere to stay," Joe said.

"No furniture to stay on, though," Julian complained.

"I can't believe I own a 12-bedroom estate, and we are sleeping on the floor of an apartment above an antique store," I sighed.

"Well, actually, you technically don't own it. Me and my wife own it!" Julian stated.

"But I inherited it!" I shouted.

"You don't deserve it!" he screamed at me.

"Stop! I know it's a difficult time right now, but you just need to calm down," Joe said.

"Remember the man from your dreams?" Julian whispered into my ear.

"What do you know about that?!" I questioned.

"I was the one in your house! Then, before I left, I drugged you so that you would suffer! I knew you were being given my house. My life! So, I just wanted you to suffer for it!" he laughed.

"That's insane! Why did you create a world just for me, then try and drug me to make me feel insane?" I screeched.

"Like I said, I gave you to Patricia so you would have a better life! I only drugged you because I knew it would help lead you to the mirror," he stated.

"Of course, that's the only reason!" I screamed. "You know what? If I'm from the other side of the mirror, then why am I trying to fix this world? You can figure out how to do it on your own! I'm going to enjoy the merging worlds! I know that Granny will never be able to get back through, but you know she did lie to me for my whole childhood."

"Lucas wait! What about all the other people who have been torn from the world? Are you just going to forget about them?!" Joe asked.

"I didn't ask for this, so like I said, Julian can figure it out! Are you coming, Joe?" I asked.

"No. You may not care, but they are still my family. And I'm going to save them!" he announced.

"Fine. It's not like we are actually related anyway," I said.

I went back down the ladder and to the car, where I planned to sleep for the night.

Time had flown by last night; what felt like 5 minutes of sleep had actually been 9 hours.

I am still happy that I walked out on Joe and Julian; the fact is, I will help them if they ask me with a plan! I need to know what I've got to do and get, but I will not be thrown around finding out that I'm not even from the same world as them! Everything seemed to be getting more confusing, more chaotic, and more miserable!

Now that I don't have anything to do... well, I don't have anything to do.

It would have been perfect, a day to me, but...

"Quick grab him!" a nearby voice shouted.

"Slash the tyres!" another voice said.

I looked around left and right, but I couldn't see anyone. I could feel the air from the tyres deflating, but no one was there to slash them. Everything went dark like a bag was over my head, and I felt like I was being dragged away with nobody there to do so!

"Hello!" I shouted. "What's going on?"

"Just be patient! Don't worry; we are not here to hurt you but instead to save you!" one voice said.

"Then why did you put a bag over my head and slash my car tyres?" And why can't I see you?" I questioned.

"Do you know about the merging worlds?" they asked.

"Well obviously! Look around us!" I shouted.

This was a very weird conversation I seemed to be having due to me talking to the air and being dragged by nothing but still being able to hear them.

"Okay… You can remove the bag from your head now," they said.

"How do you want me to remove a bag I can't even see?!" I questioned angrily.

"Fine, we'll do it for you!" they replied.

Once my vision was clear once again, I found myself sitting on a chair I could not move from in an empty closet with a little rubber duck in the corner. The rubber duck wasn't important, but it was adorable.

"Erm… Why can't I move?" I asked frustratedly.

"We've tied you to the chair... We kind of forgot you couldn't see," they said.

"You really are the worst kidnappers, aren't you?" I sighed. "It's just my luck to be kidnapped by the most stupid people ever!"

"Okay, enough of that now!" they shouted. "You know you are from our world, yes?"

"Yes, I only found out yesterday, so I don't know every little thing," I replied.

"Well, basically, due to you being born in our world and spending your whole life in what you call the real world, now that the mirror has stopped working properly, you are split into two," they told me.

"What...? I think I'm still in one piece," I said.

"So, you are two people. You are slowly fading back into our world, meaning that we can see you here, and anyone else can see you there," they explained.

"Huh, that's not worrying at all. So anyone could just attack me or kidnap me, and I wouldn't even notice," I asked.

"We have already kidnapped you!" they stated.

"Right... That's going to be fun then, isn't it?" I said. "Well, why did you kidnap me anyway? You don't seem that bad."

"We need to reopen the mirror so our worlds can be whole again! Otherwise, everyone we know will be gone forever," they said.

"How do you even know about all the mirror stuff? I thought your world was brain-dead about the whole thing," I said.

"Well, look at it this way. You had Julian who taught you about the mirror, and because he created all of it, we also have our own version of Julian over here to help us," they said.

"Oh god, double Julian. I couldn't think of anything worse!" I laughed.

"I could think of something worse! All the worlds are collapsing, and everyone we know is dying!" one of them shouted.

"No, I still think multiple Julian's are worse," I said.

"Okay, enough games now. Let's get to the point; we need your blood and a few other things!" they said.

"I know, but there's no simple way of getting the blood out of me without hurting me!" I stated.

Without any warning, I felt a slice through my arm, and the blood was oozing out of me like a fountain.

"What the hell!" I shouted. "Like, really! What the hell?!"

"Just because you might be too much of a wuss doesn't mean we are! Our world has already lost too much, and if it takes one person's pain to save hundreds of others, then we will do whatever it takes!" they shouted.

"But that was painful!" I whimpered.

Everything went silent for a while, and no one was saying anything; my arm hadn't even been patched up. I don't think... I mean, if it had, it was invisible.

"Is anyone there?" I asked, feeling a tad bit scared.

No one replied, so my assumption is that they left me alone, tied up in an invisible rope with blood spewing out of me. These are some generous kidnappers from another world.

I couldn't see much around me in the closet; there were probably things, but it was all invisible. There was still the rubber duck in the corner that I could see, but that's all. I mean, obviously, it was still there; it wasn't exactly going to get up and walk away. I used my feet to pick it up and managed to grab it from my feet with one of my hands. Considering everything, this rubber duck could be the very thing that saves the world. Okay… a bit far, I know, but you've got to consider all options in this scenario. All options, like me breaking the invisible rope somehow!

In the last 10 days, I have found out I killed my parents, then found out I didn't, and then found out they weren't even my parents. Oh yeah, and there's another world in which somehow I have managed to be in prison in both of the worlds, and then the worlds started merging, which is when I got kidnapped and tied up with an invisible rope! I think I can just about do anything at this point!

I swung myself forward, almost falling face first, but chickened out and leaned back again, but I wasn't giving up that easily! I swung forward again, this time hitting my head against the closet door. I banged my head about eight times, probably leaving me with a concussion, but no luck... I had another idea. I swung myself back as hard as I could and managed to break the back of the chair, making the rope easy to untangle, or so I thought. If you could have watched me trying to untangle myself from the invisible rope, you wouldn't have been able to stop laughing!

When I was finally free of the rope, I searched around a bit before looking for an exit. I realised I was in an apartment building, but who's? I can only assume it must be the kidnapper's apartment, but being here could tell me who the kidnappers are.

I searched the bedroom first, as that was the room

the closet was in, but there wasn't much in there other than some basic furniture items, a bed, bedside tables, lamps, and that kind of stuff. But nothing that could help me realise who they were.

Suddenly, I heard a key rattle from the other room; they had returned! They had only left a few minutes ago; they couldn't have gone very far. I still couldn't see them, but they could see me. I found myself with seconds to hide, but where?! I don't have any time. I could go back into the cupboard, but they would notice the rope wasn't there, and I couldn't exactly tie it around myself because I couldn't see it! I just slid under the bed and hid there for now, even though that is like the most obvious place to look ever!

"Oi Jim! He's gone!" one of them shouted.

"What was that, Ricky?" the other guy, who I can only assume is Jim, shouted back.

"THE GUY WE KIDNAPPED IS GONE!" Ricky screeched.

"Gone? Where?" Jim questioned.

"I don't blooming well know!" Ricky shouted.

"Well, have you looked for him?" Jim asked.

"No, I haven't looked for him, but if we were to look for him, he wouldn't know if we were right behind him!" Ricky said before grabbing my feet and pulling me out from underneath the bed.

"Let go of me!" I shouted while trying to wriggle away.

"Think you can escape from the invisible! I would think again!" Ricky said.

I couldn't see him, but I knew he was tying my feet up, so I leaned up and punched into the air as hard as I could until I felt my fist smash into his face!

"Ricky!" Jim shouted, "what did you do!?"

At this moment in time, I did not realise exactly what I had done. I knew I had punched him, but not what Jim was talking about.

He grabbed my wrists and tied them up to the

radiator before punching me in the face about 15 times, knocking me out.

An hour later

"Ahhh," I whined.

"Your awake! Listen to me! I can let you go right now if you promise me you will try to fix the mirror! If you do that, then I will be able to undo your actions," Jim stated.

"What do you mean? Undo my actions?" I asked.

"You killed Ricky! When you punched him, he hit his head on the corner of the window ledge! It killed him! I can save him by taking him through the mirror, but only if you promise you will fix it. So will you fix it if I let you go!?" Jim asked.

"I killed him," I gasped.

"Yes. Yes. Enough whining! I can save him if you fix the mirror," he shouted.

"Okay, I'll do it! I won't be a murderer!" I exclaimed.

"Okay, good," Jim said as he untied me.

"What do I need to get?" I asked.

"Well, you know you need your blood, which we already have. You will also need only three more items: a rotting apple, a bar of pure silver, and a shard of a mirror that is at least 500 years old," he told me.

"Okay, I can understand the mirror and the bar of silver, sort of, but why the rotting apple?" I asked.

"Well, when you put it together, first the apple is mushed into a paste-like texture, then the silver is melted in, and the mirror shard is smashed into tiny pieces and mixed within. All that together gets put in the cracks of the mirror, and your blood pours over the entire thing! It's weird, but it's the only way," he stated.

"Okay..." I sighed.

I got up off the floor and left the apartment, not knowing if I was being watched or followed. Even if I was, did it really matter anymore? I decided it would be best if I went back to see Julian and Joe already, as if I don't repair that mirror, then I am technically a murderer.

It did take quite a while to walk back to the store due to my car's tyres having been slashed. But that gives me time to see everything changing around the streets.

Things had gotten much worse in the few hours I had been there; there was barely anyone left! The shops that were there—I couldn't even tell you what they were, as I don't know!

"LUCAS!" a voice shouted from ahead of me.

It was Julian! He had seen me from the shop and was calling for me! I started to run, trying to hurry, as I was getting quite anxious about the world around me.

"Julian! Things have gotten a lot worse!" I exclaimed.

"I know! There's something you need to know," he

sighed.

"What? Where's Joe?" I asked.

"That's what I wanted to tell you... He's gone, Lucas. He disappeared when I woke up this morning," Julian stated.

I could feel my face turn from a smile into a frown, but I wasn't completely upset. I knew that once the mirror was repaired, everything would be back to normal again. Hopefully…

"That's okay… We need to fix the mirror!" I said

"I hope you know not everything is going to be the same again once the mirror is repaired," Julian announced.

"What do you mean?" I asked.

"Well, no one is going to remember anything once they are back... The only way they would remember is if he was lucky enough not to have disappeared," Julian explained.

"So, he would have forgotten everything? As far as

he is going to remember, we still don't talk," I asked.

"Exactly," Julian replied.

"Oh god, why did I leave?" I whimpered.

"This isn't a good time to complain... You know you will be able to rekindle your relationship again, but right now we have to save the world," Julian explained.

"He's not going to remember Granny or our parents... Or the fact that he's not even my brother," I sobbed.

"Okay enough! The quicker we get the items to fix the mirror, the quicker we can save Joe!"

"I know… We just need my blood, a rotten apple, a bar of pure silver, and a mirror that is at least 500 years old."

"How do you know all that?!"

"Oh, I got kidnapped, killed a guy, then was let go as long as I repaired the mirror."

"What?! How did you manage that since

yesterday?!"

"They were invisible! Something to do with me slowly fading back into the other world, so they can see me, but I couldn't see them."

"Oh, how could I be so stupid? I should have remembered this was going to happen once the mirror stopped doing its thing."

"You mean you knew this was going to happen?!"

"Well, I did create the mirror!" Julian exclaimed.

"So can we stop me from fading back into that world or not?" I asked.

"No. But if you get taken into that world, it won't be long before I am the last person left in this world that actually remembers... well, anything really!"

"But you will still be able to fix the mirror, right? Even without me?"

"No, not without you! If you are no longer in this world but in another, then your blood will disappear. If you don't exist in this world, then neither does your blood, obviously. It will mean I won't have all the pieces to repair the mirror."

"Why am I so powerful? If all I am is a person stolen from inside the mirror, is there no one else's blood you can use?"

"Because you were alive before you were alive."

"That doesn't even make sense?! Am I supposed to know what you are talking about?"

"Lucas was a person before the mirror; well, his name was Hector, but still. He was a good friend of mine. Until one day he was shot by a police officer, thinking he was someone else. And I couldn't just watch him die! That's when I created the other world! I used his blood with the creation of the mirror, and when it was complete, I went through to the other world and stole you from it!"

"So, when you drugged me and I had a vision of a police officer shooting me, that was actually me? Dying…"

"I suppose…"

"So how old am I? And why am I called Lucas and not Hector?"

"You're still 28 years old, and you're called Lucas, as that was just what you were called when I got you from the other world."

"Oh okay… Well, I'm beginning to feel a bit sick, but if that's true, then we really need to hurry up before I disappear!"

"Yes, you are right; we do need to hurry! First, I say we start with the most difficult thing to get so we can work our way down to the easier stuff."

"So, the piece of a 500-year-old mirror then? I've already got the blood... I mean, it's in a bag, but I've got it."

"I probably had an old mirror we could have used in the antique shop, but that's empty now, so my next suggestion is the museum," Julian suggested.

"Yeah, that would probably work. I mean,

everyone is gone, so nobody would notice, so it should be okay," I agreed.

"Some people are still here, just not many."

"Yeah, yeah, I know. Just probably not for long."

We started off on our journey to the nearest museum, which was miles away, so it would have been easier just to steal another car, which is exactly what we did. I'm beginning to understand how I have managed to be in jail twice now.

I let Julian drive us there because, to be honest, I just wanted to chill and enjoy the journey. It was quite terrifying driving down the empty streets; it felt like a ghost town. I was growing more nervous looking at everything, at the pain the mirror had already caused. What if I can't repair it in time?

At the museum...

We arrived at the museum and went to park the car. That was one good thing about everything: parking spots everywhere.

We got out and headed over to the front entrance of the museum to try and get in. If the front door was locked, then I'm not really sure of any other entrances. Hopefully Julian knows... Although I really do expect a lot from him...

"What do we do if the door is locked?" I asked.

"We find another entrance, duh!" Julian answered.

"Yes, but do you actually know of any other entrances, just in case?" I asked.

"No, but everywhere has an escape exit, I think," he replied.

"Yeah, I suppose," I huffed.

I walked up to the front door and jiggled the handle. Yes! It was open! Finally, things were looking good for us! This could be our first sign of good luck! Or not... There was another set of doors through the first door! It must have been for extra security so people wouldn't break in. Although, who would want to break into a museum? Other than us, obviously...

The second set of doors were locked. Of course, they were! I take back everything I said about our luck looking good!

"So, what now?" I questioned.

"We walk around the side of the building and look for a side door. If we can't find an entrance, we break a window," he replied.

"What?! Since when did we go around vandalising things!?" I questioned.

"Since we almost ended the world!" Julian replied.

"Okay, fair point," I said.

I walked around the side of the building, but there weren't any doors there, so I continued going around and eventually saw a ladder hidden in a little shed. The only thing is that the ladder goes down. It probably leads to the sewers, so hopefully there is another ladder leading into the museum.

"Julian over here!" I shouted, calling Julian over from the other side of the building.

"What? You found a door in?" he asked.

"Not exactly… A ladder…" I stated.

"And how do you know that it leads into the museum?" he asked.

"Well, I don't, but it doesn't hurt to try," I shouted.

"Okay…Okay… Just go!" Julian said.

I pulled open the shed door, which snapped right off due to the rotting wood it was made from. Wooaoaoah, I felt a shiver go down my spine, probably from the number of spiders crawling around every corner. I picked up the small hatch that covered the ladder and then made my way down slowly, step by step. Julian followed, not far behind.

"OI! I'm stuck!" Julian shouted.

"How are you stuck?!" I chuckled.

"I don't know! This ladder hole is too small!" he whined.

I didn't say it before because I didn't want to be rude, but Julian was just a bit of a podge, a chunky, elephant-sized chonk. So, I really should have known beforehand that he wouldn't be able to fit down…

"Can you try going back up?" I suggested.

"I can't move!" he shouted.

"What do you want me to do?!" I asked.

"I don't know! Just go and find a way in!" Julian said in anger.

"Okay… Okay…" I said in an annoyed tone.

I walked through the tunnels trying to find another ladder up, but it wasn't long after I walked up that I realised I had walked the wrong way. So, I turned back and was once again on my way towards the museum!

I saw three ladders on my walk: the first one leading to the middle of the road, the second one leading underneath a large bin, and the third one leading me into the bin rooms of the museum! Not exactly where I wanted to be, but I'm in!

I pushed open the door from the bin room into the

main museum, which is when I saw security guards! Really?! Out of the few people there are left in the world, there are still security guards!

Now I had to try and be sneaky to steal the mirror when I had planned to just walk in and take it before.

I hid behind a wall near the door to the garbage room and waited for security to pass by. They seemed to just stand around, like they were waiting for me to jump out and shout, "Hey, I'm over here." I had to take action and do something, as just standing around waiting was getting boring now.

I went back into the garbage room and looked for another entrance. There was a vent, but I think I would suffocate in it.

Suddenly, the door swung open, and a security guard walked in.

"Oh… I'm so sorry. Um, I'll leave just… I'll leave!" I freaked.

He didn't reply or even look at me.

"Hello?" I said. "Huh? So, you can't hear me then?"

Well, this suddenly just got a whole lot easier. I just walked straight out past him and throughout the museum, like I was invisible. Oh… This probably meant I had faded out more! If I don't hurry, I will be completely gone!

I started running, and like those cool scenes in a movie, I began disappearing into grey clouds of murky smoke!

I was gone.

Okay, I'm sorry, that was a bit dramatic. I am still alive, but just in the other world now. I'm still in the museum, like nothing has changed, but in this world, I'm all by myself.

I stood still for a while, as I didn't really know what to do next. I know I need to get everything together still, but I feel a bit lost without being told what to do by Julian. And the bag of blood I had would have disappeared! Now I need to do that again as well!

"OI GUYS, WE'VE GOT A TRESPASER!" a security guard shouted.

"You can see me now?!" I questioned.

"See you now? What kind of question is that?" the guard replied.

I must have gotten it wrong before! I thought because I was fading into this world and they were in the normal world that they couldn't see me, but no. I could only see them because they were in what I'm now going to call MY world when I was fading in.

Confusing, but sort of makes sense, right?

"Why do people think they have the right to just let themselves into private property?" the guard asked another guard.

With my hands stuck down by my side, I suddenly felt something in my pocket: the rubber duck from Jim and Ricky's closet (The Kidnappers)! Although it felt like there was something inside of it, it felt like a key of some sort! Probably a spare one in case Ricky or Jim ever got locked in themselves. With great difficulty, I used my hand to try and rip it through a little hole in the mouth of the duck. Yes! I have the key! But what to do with the key? Or what not to do with the key?

"Hey! I've got a knife in my pocket." I lied to the security guard.

Don't worry, I have a plan.

The guard wrestled my hands down by my side, then had to decide which of my hands to let go of to check my pocket. He chose the one furthest away from the pocket I had said the knife was in, but the key was in the other pocket. I mean, how stupid can they be?

"I'm sorry!" I yelled as I stabbed the key into his neck.

"AGGGHHH!" he shrieked, falling to his back.

I got up off the floor and began running away, then

I stopped and turned back to see if he was still chasing me.

He was gone. Not gone like he had crawled away, but gone as in gone... Nothing... Dead...

Looking at where he had been lying, I noticed in the corner of my eye a mirror bolted to the wall. The exact kind I was looking for... convenient. I began walking up to it slowly until a black goo came running down the wall from behind it, slowly creeping towards me. I backed up quicker and quicker until I was met with a wall. It surrounded me like an army of hungry lions, and then something began to emerge from within...

A shard of the mirror itself... It's almost like it knew exactly what I needed, and it was gifting it to me.

"Okay... thanks, I guess," I said in a confused tone.

I stepped over the black goo and serenely walked away, continuously looking back behind me after every step. This was suddenly a lot simpler than I expected. I didn't even know if I would find a mirror that was over 500 years old. I still don't know if I did. Technically, I never got a chance to check if it was over 500 years old, but I will just assume for now...

I left through the front doors of the museum as I could open them from the inside, and that's when I saw a familiar face.

"Granny!" I shouted in excitement. "How did you know I was going to be here?"

"I will always know where you are, Little Lukey," she said with a smile.

SCCRREEEEEEEEEEEEEEEEEEEEEEEEEEEEEEEEE EEEEEEEEEEEEEEEEEEEEEEEEEEEEEEEEEEEEEEE EEEEEEEEEEEECCCCCCCHHHHHHHHH!

A loud screech noise echoed around me like a tornado of madness!

"AHHHH! Can you not hear that?!" I asked Granny.

"Hear what, Luke?" she asked.

"That loud screeching sound!" I exclaimed.

"Did Julian explain to you about..." she began saying.

"Me being someone called Hector and not related to you at all, or that it wasn't actually you who killed Mum and Dad, what? Is that what you were going to ask?" I questioned in a sudden rush of aggression.

"Luke I'm sorry... But that screeching noise only you can hear because it's the world dying," she said.

"Great! Just great! So now, not only am I this old, dead, young, and alive person, but I can also hear the world dying! Not even the real world—a world through a magical mirror. Just amazing!" I bellowed.

"Well, at least your life doesn't get boring," Granny grinned.

"Boring! Are you trying to joke with me right now?! I am getting bored of all this nonsense!" I shouted.

"Stop shouting at me!" Granny yelled. "I am still

your grandmother, and you do not talk to me like that!" she scolded.

"Look, I'm sorry, okay... It's just a lot," I whimpered.

"I know… and I'm sorry I never told you when you were younger, but I was scared for you," she explained.

"Okay. We need to stop now. We are wasting too much time. Let's get on with it!" I said.

"How bad is the other world?" Granny asked.

"Julian is all that's left," I told her.

"We really don't have much time... It really depends on how strong you are now; you are the vessel of the world. The more pain the world feels, you will start to feel it, and eventually, if you can't handle it anymore, then it's all gone. The real world will be healed if this one is gone, but you will be gone for good. And I hate to say this, Luke, but no one will have even remembered you existed, not even me," she sobbed.

"Okay, let's go back to the house, maybe... If you still have the house, that is," I inquired.

"Of course I do. What do you not have the house in the other world?" she asked in a panic.

"No... I mean, they're probably gone now, but there was someone else who had the house for some reason," I said.

"Oh... okay..." she said with a look of dismay.

We then ventured on towards the house with the new information I had found out, and I was in glee that I had accomplished finding the mirror shard.

"Granny. When looking for the mirror piece I needed, this goo came out from beneath it and pretty much just passed me a shard of the mirror, like it knew I needed it. Which makes me sound crazy," I said, doubting myself.

"No, that is exactly what it is doing, and it needs to stop! Although it is helpful that the world is trying to help its owner, it's draining your energy without meaning to! You need to control it!" she exclaimed.

"Control it! Easier said than done," I sighed.

"I know. It will get easier, I promise," she smiled.

Although I know she was trying to be nice, it actually made me feel worse because even if I did get us through this, it would just go back to how it was. Granny is living here with my parents, Joe is ignoring me, and I am all alone again.

When I arrived back home, I had a sudden sigh of relief to be back in the house—no, to be back home. I sat down on the living room sofa and just took a second to take in everything. Maybe a bit longer than just a second, I may have fallen asleep...

"Um, excuse me. Wake up," came a voice.

I rubbed my eyes until I could see clearly, and then, full of enjoyment, I yelled, "Mum!"

"No. Look, my mum told us a bit about you hitting your head and getting new, weird memories, so I will let you stay for a while, but you have to call me by my first name, Tia," she said.

"Hit my head. Oh, okay," I sighed.

"Is he awake yet?" my dad asked, walking in from the kitchen.

"Dad!" I shouted.

"No. It's Steve!" he stated.

"Oh okay…" I frowned.

"How are you feeling now?" Steve asked.

"What do you mean? I feel fine," I said in a confused tone.

"Oh, my mother-in-law told me you had been through a lot... So, I was just asking if you are, okay?" Steve said.

"Oh. Yeah, I think I'm okay," I said.

"What's that supposed to mean? You think you're okay?" Steve asked.

"Sorry, I do think I need to get going now. I have a lot to do," I said eagerly.

"No! At least stay for a tea," Tia begged.

"Alright, I could never turn down a tea," I grinned.

It felt odd being asked to stay for a cup of tea by my parents, considering they had been trying to throw me out before. I wonder why they are being so welcoming now.

Not much later, my mum brought me a tea, and we all went and sat around the dining table, trying to have a conversation. When I say trying, it's because they were definitely trying to make time pass by, but why?

"Look. I am really enjoying talking to you both, but I have something I need to do, so I think I'm going to head off now," I said.

"No, you have to stay for some lunch!" Tia offered.

"She does make a good lunch," Steve stated.

"Why are you trying to keep me here?" I questioned.

"We're not..." Tia said.

"Okay, then I'm going to leave now," I stated.

"Alright fine! Patricia told us to keep you here! We don't know why, but that's what she said before leaving. And before you ask, no, we don't know where she went," Steve said.

"Well, I'm leaving now," I stated before stomping off.

Why would Granny want me to be kept here?

As I walked away, I noticed something missing—the shard of the mirror!

"Hey!" I shouted back. "Where's the mirror shard?"

"We don't know about a mirror shard, but Granny did leave with a bag," Tia mentioned.

Unexpectedly, a sudden smell arose from behind the house, like a bonfire had just started. I sprinted towards the kitchen window, with my mum and dad following, not too far behind. Outside, I witnessed Granny throwing old bits of wood and twigs into a huge fire. There it was. The mirror shard in the centre of it all...

"GRANNY, STOP!" I charged into the garden and yelled.

"I'm sorry, Lukey, but this is for your own good," she said.

"How?! How is this for my own good?" I asked

angrily.

"We might not have much time left... I want to spend it as a family. I'm sorry, Luke, but I don't think you can save us. I don't believe in you," she sobbed.

This felt worse than being stabbed by Julian; it made me weak, and it made this world weak. It felt like I was watching myself go up in flames; by destroying what I needed to fix the mirror, she was killing me.

I took a step towards the flames, ready to be submerged within; after all, I was going to disappear anyway. Every step closer I took, I felt calmer, happier, and freer. But the world wouldn't free me that easily; the fire vanished into thin air, and I dropped to the pile of sticks with a crunch!

I didn't feel any pain from the fire; I was in pain from the looks around me, the anger in my dad's eyes, the frightened look on my mum's face, and Granny's hope slowly leaving her.

"Luke…" Granny stuttered.

"I don't want to hear it, Patricia!" I yelled.

I grabbed the mirror shard from the middle of where the fire had been and headed straight towards the garden wall. This is my world. I can do as I please!

The wall exploded open towards the streets beyond. I have the shard of the mirror again, my blood is easy to acquire again, and now I just need the last two items. The apple and the bar of pure silver.

I had a new sense of power, like I could do and be anything I wanted to. So onwards, I went towards… Well, I don't know yet, but I'm going somewhere.

Where could I get a bar of pure silver?

I would say the antique store again, but I'm pretty sure that's probably empty even in this world. Oh well, it's somewhere to go.

The antique store really isn't far from the house, so it will take me no time to arrive there, especially considering I can move and destroy anything around me.

The antique store (IN MY WORLD)

Wow, it looks so... exactly the same. Boring. And it was empty, just like the one in the other world.

"WHHHHHHHHYYYYYYY!? I JUST WANT MY LIFE BACK!" I screamed into the air, under the impression that no one could hear me.

"I can help you with that," said a familiar voice from behind the counter of the antique shop.

"Julian?" I said, assuming it was him.

I suppose there is the original Julian, the mirror Julian, and now a merging-worlds version of Julian. Hopefully more helpful than past Julians.

"So, your Lucas, then? I've heard some rumours about you," he said.

"Oh right. You don't technically know me in this world... What kind of rumours?" I asked.

"Well, I haven't actually heard any rumours, but I just wanted to sound cool," he frowned.

"You definitely are just a mirror replica of the other Julian, aren't you?" I laughed.

"I don't know… I've never met the other Julian," he said angrily.

"O…k… Do you happen to have a bar of silver I can have?" I straight up asked.

"Look around you! Does it look like I have anything left?!" he shouted.

"Jeez. It was just a question," I shouted.

"We don't have time for just a question! I'm assuming if the other Julian taught you anything that you are trying to repair the mirror," he asked.

"Um, yes," I replied.

"What parts have you got so far?" he questioned.

"I have the 500-year-old shard of a mirror; I am my own blood, so I suppose I've already got that, and now all that's left is the rotting apple and the bar of pure silver," I said.

"Okay, so why are we just standing around then?

Let's get a move on!" he hurried.

"Where are we going?" I asked.

"Where do you think?" he asked back.

"Well, I don't know... Otherwise, I wouldn't ask. Clearly!"

"Just get in the car, and I'll take you there."

I got into Julian's car with no knowledge of where he was going to take me, but I have to say I do prefer the other Julian. Even if he did stab me...

"WAIT, STOP THE CAR!" I yelled.

I saw something as we were driving—a lamp post with a sign on it. The sign just said, 'This Way' with an arrow pointing back up the street we had just driven down. Usually, I wouldn't think anything of a random sign, but there was a certain bubble of energy surrounding it that made me know in that moment that this sign was the world trying to help me again.

"We need to turn around and go back," I told Julian.

"What no! I know where we can get the silver!" Julian exclaimed.

"Yes, I know, but just trust me when I tell you we need to go back!" I shouted.

"Okay, but if this is for no reason, I am not going to be happy!" he stated.

We turned the car around and continued back up the road we had just come down. Eventually, we passed the antique store again, but I still felt like we had to keep going further. Then, randomly, out of nowhere, the car broke down outside of a little flower shop. I took this as a sign of where we needed to be.

"So, what now, Mr Know It All?" Julian asked rudely.

"In here," I said, pointing to the flower shop.

"A flower shop? What do you expect to find in there?" he asked.

"Well, hopefully, the silver..." I replied.

"In a flower shop?" he asked, trying not to laugh.

"Let's just have a look, and we will see after that, okay?" I said.

"Whatever," he huffed.

I went into the shop hoping to find the silver sitting on the side waiting for me, but no, I couldn't see it anywhere! Maybe all of those signs were just signs! I searched every crevice of the shop and every flower petal. I even started ripping up some floorboards, but the best I found was an old penny!

What was the point!? I walked out of the shop where Julian was waiting in the car for me, and it wasn't until I got back in the car that he mentioned something to me.

"So, you find anything after making me follow them signs?" he asked.

"NO!" I yelled in anger.

"Well, did you manage to get the wrong side of the road by any chance?" he asked.

"What do you mean?" I questioned.

I looked across the street from the flower shop, and there it was. Not the silver, but what would hold the silver? A Bank. If I could get into there, then it surely would hold the silver! Yet, although there's not really many people left around to care about me robbing a bank, they still have high security in the building, security cameras, sensory lasers (lasers that can sense you), and the building could instantly lock down and trap me, as well as more stuff I probably don't know about.

"Wait, did you know about the bank the whole time I was in the flower shop?" I asked.

"Well yeah, but it was quite funny; you thought it was in a flower shop," he laughed.

"I hate you," I said.

I got out of the car and walked over to the front doors of the bank, which I knew would be locked, but that wouldn't be a problem for me. Not anymore.

Craaack... The ground beneath my feet rumbled

through step after step. *Craack!* The world knew the pain I was about to put it through. Breaking into a bank will use a lot of my energy, if not all my energy. If I can't handle it, then the world will crumble beneath my very feet. The cracks I have created are trying to warn me.

I reached my hand out and felt the cold touch of the brass door handle. Obviously, I knew it wouldn't be open, so I closed my eyes and thought to myself, if I can control a world, then this door will very well be unlocked when I open my eyes! As I began to see daylight, I gave the door another push, but this time it swung open as calmly as a feather. I was in.

Now to try and figure out how to get through without setting alarms off, as even though no one will come running, it would just be really annoying.

BBBGBG...

HGBGGHBGBG...

BGGHHGBGB...

The ground shook beneath my feet before a sinkhole opened straight through the middle of the bank. I know this is a result of me using energy, which is destroying the world, but now I am going to have to use it to cross the hole!

Or maybe not.

I have to get around somehow, but maybe there is a hallway or something I could go through.

Nope.

It's much easier for me to just use my magical power stuff to get over it.

Or maybe not again.

I think I can just jump across the hole; I mean, it's not too far, and if I do fall, it will only hurt a little bit. Well, sure, let's say a little bit. So here I go, ready to jump. 3…2…1 and **JUMP!** I leapt over the hole, and I felt my toes touch the other side, but then just as glee filled me, it quickly deteriorated as I fell backwards and tumbled down! As I rapidly fell to what I assumed would be my demise, I was snatched by the ground as it grew beneath me and assisted in a soft landing.

"Are you okay down there?" Julian shouted.

"DO I LOOK OK?!" I yelled.

"Okay, do you want help or not?" he asked.

"Knowing you, you'll just make things worse!" I shouted.

"If you don't want my help, I will just go back to the car," he stated.

"No. I'm sorry. Please help me," I sighed.

"Can't you just ask the world to help you out?" he asked.

"It doesn't quite work like that... Well, I guess it does, but it also slowly destroys the universe," I replied.

"Okay, well, I think I've got an old rope in the back of my car I can use to get you out," he offered.

"Why do you have a rope in the back of your car?" I asked.

"Well, you never know when someone whose life could destroy our world may get stuck in a sinkhole," he smirked.

"Okay, okay, just get the rope, please," I requested.

He went to the car to grab it for me, but by the time he got back, I had managed to climb out, as it seemed to be that I actually wasn't that deep down.

"You took your time, didn't you?" I said.

"How did you get out so easily?" Julian asked.

"I just climbed. It really wasn't that deep," I answered.

"So, what do I do now?" Julian asked.

"You could jump over and help me?" I suggested.

"No, I think I'm just going to wait in the car," he said before walking away.

"Okay then…" I muttered to myself.

Where do I go next?

I had managed to get across to the cash registers, but that should have been the easy part if the sinkhole hadn't formed. Now I have to find a way to the vault. There was a sealed door behind the cash register, but I couldn't open that if I wanted to. I mean, I could, but I really need to stop; otherwise, I will destroy the world.

"AHHHHH! AHHHHHHHHH!" I screeched.

The pain I felt was like a trillion knives twisting inside of me!

"AHHHHHHHHHHH!" I yelled again.

Julian came running in and yelled, "Are you okay? What's going on!?"

"AHHH! What is this pain?" I screamed.

"Oh! You've been expecting too much help from the world! Not only the world will feel pain, but you will too," he explained.

"I can do this! I can—I can—I can do it!" I stuttered, almost passing out.

"No, you need to sit!" Julian shouted.

"NO! I CAN DO THIS!" I yelled.

I stood up with all the might I had, tore the metal door right off its hinges, and threw it across the room, smashing it into a wall.

"THIS IS MY WORLD, AND I WILL DO WHAT I WANT!" I shrieked.

"You're just going to do more damage!" Julian shouted at me.

I turned around and looked Julian in the eyes and said, "Shut up!" before covering his mouth with my hand and removing his voice completely!

"CAHHChAh…" he tried talking.

"MY WORLD!" I said again.

I stormed down the stairs behind where the metal door once was, and there it was. The vault! I had no trouble opening it with the strength I had found within myself.

Mountains of gold and cash surrounded the room, and a table of silver bars was pushed to the corner. Finally, I had three of the items I needed, and now all

I needed was a rotting apple, which I could probably find in Julian's car!

A sudden breeze swept upon me, leaving me as pale as a polar bear and as weak as an ant, like the energy I had felt had now passed by. I dropped to my knees, barely being able to breathe, and there I lay for what seemed to be hours. Eventually, Julian came down the stairs to see what was taking me so long.

"That strength didn't last long, did it?" he said.

"How are you ta-ta-talking?" I shivered.

"Oh, you became weak, and my voice just reappeared with you not having the energy to keep it with you!" he said.

"He—help me," I begged.

"Hah. Help you. Even if you hadn't stolen my voice and betrayed me like 5 minutes ago, I still wouldn't have helped you," he laughed.

"Why? Why would you do that?" I asked.

"Because you have just helped me gather the few

materials to create my own world! All I needed was the bar of silver and the 500-year-old shard of mirror from you! Then I have the frame of a mirror from over 1000 years ago and my own blood, which is what I will need to create my world! Once I have what I want, all the other worlds can rot in hell!" he explained.

"Why? You will kill billions of people just to control your own world?!" I questioned.

"Do you know how it feels to be the other Julian? The guy in the shadows with no one to talk to and nothing to do but sit around in an antique shop all day?!" he asked.

"If you felt like that, why didn't you come through the mirror in the first place? You could have come to our world," I said.

"Your grandmother would never let me in to see the mirror; she always hated me! She only ever loved the other world Julian; even though I am exactly the same, I will always be an outcast! Well, now she will pay! Pay with your life!" he yelled.

"What? What do you mean?!" I screamed.

"I'm going to burn you alive! And if your precious world saves you, then I'm pretty sure that will push you past your breaking point and destroy everything anyway!" he laughed as he walked off, dropping a lit match behind him.

The carpet went up in flames surrounding me, growing closer by the second, and yes, he was right. I can't save myself. This time, I really can't do anything. I could tell the world was trying to help me keep the fire off, but all it was doing was destroying itself and me.

I think it is time to accept my fate.

I awoke with a jolt. But at least I awoke... But where I was is another question.

"Um... Hello..." I shouted.

"Lucas, you are supposed to have repaired the mirror by now! Ricky is still dead!" Jim shouted.

"Jim? You're still here!" I said in excitement, "and you have a face!"

"Yes, I did technically have a face the whole time; you just couldn't see it... and, of course, I'm still here! I'm stronger than all the other morons being ripped away!" he stated.

"Okay, how did you know where to find me? I mean, I was in a burning bank," I asked.

"I have my ways, and I was just following you the whole time," he said.

"You were? And I didn't even notice... creepy," I whimpered.

"Nope, you were pretty oblivious," he smirked.

"Okay, but we have bigger problems! Julian has stolen all the items I needed to repair the mirror to create his own!"

"Oh. And you wait until now to tell me!?"

"When else did you want me to tell you? When I was passed out from the fumes of the fire?! Which also thanks for saving my life and all that!"

"You should have told me from the moment you woke up! And you're welcome."

"So, what do we do now?"

We both sat in silence contemplating what we should do next, as neither of us knew where he could be or if he'd already created the mirror to a new world.

"What about if we kill him?" Jim asked.

"What!? No, we can't!" I shrieked.

"Why? You did kill Ricky. What's another dead guy?" Jim said.

"Oh my god! That was an accident! I couldn't even see him!" I yelled.

"Sure, sure, whatever you say," he grunted.

"Okay fine! Let's say we do kill him. What do we do after that?" I asked.

"We take the items and repair the mirror!" Jim stated.

"Okay. I guess that's the best idea we've got. Let's do it!" I said in encouragement.

I got up and left outside before turning around to Jim with one small question that might be useful to get Julian...

"How are we planning on killing Julian?" I asked.

I thought that might be quite an important

question, considering it's the whole plan.

"I don't know... with a knife?" he suggested.

"Okay, but that seems too easy for it to work," I stated.

"Well, we'll decide once we find him! OK!?" he shouted.

"Okay fine!" I said.

We had also agreed on checking the antique store first, as that is where he usually turns up in either of the worlds. We had to walk there, though, which was actually quite useful as it meant I could ask some questions.

"What happens if he's already created the new mirror to a new world?" I asked.

"Well, then we will really be running out of time to get everything again to repair this mirror!" Jim said.

"And what if he hasn't managed to create the mirror? Do we just take the items back?" I questioned.

"Well, that was the plan—to kill him and take the

items back," Jim said in an irritated tone.

"I suppose, but I just have a bad feeling about this," I sighed.

"Well, then something probably has already happened. Trust me, I'm sure you'll know when a new world opens," he told me.

I trusted what he said, and we continued onward towards the antique store. I still felt a lot of pain from the world, but not as bad as in the bank.

"Looking for me?" Julian said, standing on top of a car in the middle of the street.

"JULIAN! Why are you in the middle of the street? You know what? Never mind; you need to stop whatever you are doing! I promise, once we fix this mirror, I will help you," I shouted.

"Help me! No! I want the power now! I want the freedom! You really thought I wanted your help! Pathetic!" he laughed.

"Hey, let's all be calm here and talk this through

like adults," Jim suggested.

"Oh, but it's so much more fun rubbing it in your faces! Lucas, you literally helped me get the items for my world by destroying your own! So, if you think about it, I've done nothing wrong!" Julian grinned.

"I was trying to save the world; actually, I was trying to save two worlds! At once!" I shouted.

"Yes, but only for your own selfish needs! You just wanted to fix everything to sell your grandmother's house for money! Then what? Were you just going to destroy the mirror after?" he questioned.

"How... How did you know I was going to sell Granny's house? And what makes you think I would destroy the mirror and not take it with me?" I asked.

"I have my ways of finding things out, Lucas, and of course, you wouldn't have taken the mirror with you! You would have killed everyone inside if it meant your safety!" Julian hissed.

"Wait, but if Lucas destroys the mirror, he will

suffer as well. That's why he's trying to save it," Jim mentioned.

"Yeah, exactly why would I destroy it?" I asked.

"Oh enough! This world will be gone soon anyway! If you want to witness the creation of my new world, then you will be at the house by nightfall!" he shouted before walking off into the distance.

"Wait, what house?" I tried shouting at him.

"He probably means his house," Jim said.

"No, he doesn't have a house... He lives in an apartment above the antique shop," I said.

"Well, maybe your house then?" he suggested.

"Yeah, I suppose. Although he said Granny didn't like him, I don't know how he would get in," I questioned.

"That should be the least of our worries right now. The question is, What do we do next?" Jim asked.

"Well, we could go to the house... No?" I asked

"Yes, but what then? He will be expecting us to

turn up; we need a plan," Jim stated.

It took us a while of pacing up and down the streets, thinking one idea after another, until we finally arrived at the perfect plan!

"I've got it!" I shouted.

"Got what?" Jim asked.

"Well, a plan, obviously!" I replied.

"Yes, okay, but what is the plan?" he asked.

"Okay, so you're going to set one of the outside hedges on fire to distract Julian while I sneak in and steal the items?" I suggested.

"That is one of the stupidest plans I have ever heard, but it might just work," he agreed.

"Okay. Then what are we waiting for? Let's go!" I shouted.

Unless he has already created the mirror by the time we get there, then, in that case, we are screwed.

So, off we went again towards the place I always seem to end up, Granny's house.

"How do you plan on setting the fire?" I asked Jim.

"With a match... or a lighter. Or whatever I find along the way," he said.

"Okay, but that won't set it off very fast. We could grab some petrol from a petrol station and use that," I suggested.

"We can, I suppose, but where is the nearest petrol station?" he asked.

"I don't actually know. Probably a couple of miles away," I said.

"So, you want us to walk miles to walk all the way back just to set a fire?" he asked.

"Okay. Well, you got any better ideas on what we can use to make the fire bigger?" I asked.

"Actually, I do. I know it will hurt a lot, but what if you can use your world power stuff to make it grow?" he said.

"I suppose I could, but it will make the world deteriorate a lot faster!"

"Yes, but if we can get the stuff from him anyway, then it shouldn't matter because we can just repair the mirror."

"I guess…"

We soon arrived at the bottom of the driveway leading up to the house.

Breathe in and breathe out. Breathe in and breathe out. I slowly sank into a pit of panic when I arrived. This may have been because the doors were flat down on the floor where they had been broken off, windows were smashed all around, and I couldn't hear or see Granny or my parents anywhere.

"Jim, are you ready?" I asked slowly, taking a moment to prepare.

"I think so," he replied in a voice of true fear, "are you?"

"Yeah… Yeah, I think so," I mumbled.

We both very much did not want to do this, but it was quite literally a life-or-death scenario. Jim dropped a match on the hedges outside, and already the fire grew larger and larger, but with all I could, I made it form a massive ring around the house. It grew taller by the second, too tall. I walked into the house with Jim waiting out the front, and there I greeted Granny, tied up to a chair!

"Granny! What happened to you?" I screeched.

"Julian! Who did you think!? Untie me, please!" she demanded.

"Where is he?" I asked.

"I'll tell you if you untie me!" she stated.

"And I'll untie you if you tell me!" I replied.

"FINE! He's upstairs in the attic! Now untie me at once!" she demanded.

"You know what? I think I'll leave you here until I know for sure," I said.

"YOU WILL LET ME OUT THIS INSTANT BOY!" Granny screeched.

I continued up the staircase, ignoring her every

word, but it wasn't long before I was greeted by Julian once again.

"Why do you always have to walk off?" I asked. "You never just stay put!"

"Why do you always have to follow me?" he replied with a question.

"Okay, enough now. Where's the new mirror?" I asked.

"It's in the process of being created. Not that I'm going to let you get near it!" he said.

"When you say in the process, do you mean already created or almost ready to create?" I asked.

He took a step towards me and whispered in my ear, "Already created! Now it will crumble the rest of the worlds along with you and everyone else."

"You really think so? I would look out the window!" I stated.

He walked over to the window and began laughing.

"Why are you laughing?" I asked.

"Because the fire will just help destroy this world faster! Starting with this house!" he said.

"What's that supposed to mean?" I asked.

I walked over to the window and looked outside myself; the fire had erupted up the side of the house and was rapidly submerging it within! How could I have not thought this was going to happen?!

"What? Can you not make the fire disappear? No, of course not. You're just as weak as any mortal being, aren't you?" he laughed.

I tried barging past him to go to the attic, where the mirror was, and he didn't even try to stop me; in fact, he moved out of my way! I didn't question this but instead continued on towards the attic, and there it was! Even more majestic than the other mirror! But I must destroy it! But how?

"So, what are you going to do with it now?" Julian asked.

"Well, clearly, it's not usable at the moment; otherwise, I would have crossed over to the other side, so I guess I will just let it burn in the fire," I said.

"It's a mirror; it's not going to burn!" Julian exclaimed.

"Yes, but once the house collapses down on itself, surely it will smash into a million pieces anyway!" I stated.

"There's another world being created in there! You think a small fall will destroy it?!"

"I don't know then," I muttered, slowly losing faith in myself.

"Look, I have an offer for you. Go and sit with your grandmother downstairs and just enjoy your time together before the house collapses on you and the world is destroyed, or you can continue trying to destroy the mirror and die anyway," Julian offered.

"Okay. You win," I said.

You didn't really think I was going to give up that

easily, did you? No, of course not! I did go downstairs to Granny, though, because I had to say something to her just in case everything... Stops.

"Um... Granny..." I said.

"Calling me Granny again, are we? If I remember correctly, after you stormed out, it was Patricia; you called me! My first name!" she sneered.

"Okay, I'm sorry, but you were trying to destroy all hope of me saving the mirror," I said.

"Well, you still didn't manage to fix it, did you?" she said.

"I'm working on it!" I said angrily. "Just listen to me! I am going to do something that might kill me, but if I manage to save the mirror, you will need to go back home. You can't live in this world anymore; I don't think I will be able to save this world as well as the real world. Just the real world."

"Well, don't bother then! I won't lose this world! I only came here to be with my family, and now you expect me to go back and just act like they were always dead?! I won't!" she said.

"Okay, then goodbye, granny," I said one last time.

CRRRAASH!

The ceiling came caving down to the first floor as fire burst through the house. I didn't have much time left! I had to run! This wasn't my plan, but if I don't leave now, then no one will make it out alive! From every direction I looked, fire was there. Every window was covered, every door was blocked, and any safe spots were gone!

I know if I use my power, I will be freed, but I can feel that if I use it, the world will crumble by the second. But that was my only option, or I could die, which would destroy the world either way.

I closed my eyes and walked forward towards the open door of flames. The closer I got, the hotter it was, and I couldn't feel anything moving away. It wasn't working. I wasn't strong enough anymore. This is it.

I refuse to go out without a fight! I stormed up the stairs as fast as I could, dodging the fire with every step. If I wanted to go back down now, it wouldn't be possible.

"Julian stop!" I shouted.

"Stop what?" he asked. "You started this fire! Remember? Well, now you all go down with it!"

"You realise you will die as well?" I said.

"Oh no, I won't, though. You see, although these windows are high, I will get out completely fine!" he exclaimed.

"That's not possible," I said.

"Oh yeah, look out the window!" he said.

I walked over and looked out the massive window, looking over the tiny bit there was left of the world, but I couldn't see what he was talking about.

"What do you want me to see?" I asked.

"NOTHING!" he shouted as he pushed me through it, leaving me falling to my doom. "You see,

I won't be able to get out, but at least I won something!"

Crash! I crashed into a pile of leaves created by Jim. He had saved me!

"QUICK, GET UP!" Jim shouted, "THE HOUSE IS ABOUT TO CRASH DOWN!"

I jumped up as fast as I could, but not fast enough. I charged forward, trying to get out of the way, but I failed! The top of the chimney from the roof hit my legs and knocked me down!

I awoke alone in the middle of the street, this time without anyone waking me.

I stood from the crumbled ashes of the house, and I didn't know what I expected, but it was all gone. The house, everything... AND JULIAN! I don't know how he got out, but he did! But right now, I have a bigger problem...

"JIM!" I shouted. "Where are you?!"

I searched through the rubble that was left, underneath anything he could be under, and I found him. I found him. Well, I'll leave it at that.

I may not have known him for long, and we may have met because he kidnapped me, but he had already saved my life once and was trying to help me save the world.

"Goodbye, my friend..."

I picked up the broken mirror that I had still failed to repair and walked down to the antique store. The same place I always go when I look for Julian; if there is any chance I can destroy the mirror, then I'm going to take it!

The plan originally was to just kill Julian so he wouldn't have the chance to create the mirror, but as he had already done it, our plan became invalid. So now my plan is to trap him in his own creation! How do I plan on doing that, you ask? By putting him in between the reflections of two magical mirrors! Hopefully, it will tear him apart, and I'm hoping that in doing so, it will use the energy from his mirror to repair mine!

Now obviously I won't be able to just walk in, especially holding the mirror, so I plan to offer to help him with the energy his mirror will require, then strike after that!

I suddenly felt really pumped full of energy. I can do this! He doesn't stand a chance with me against him! I've got this far, and all I can say now is...

Let's do this!

I began to run down the street to the store and got there in minutes! But he wasn't here for the first time ever!

Where could he be, then?

I tried thinking back to remember if there was anywhere else he might be, but I couldn't think of anywhere else.

Unless he was here...

The thought crossed my mind quite randomly, but it actually would make sense; he may be on the roof of the shop. It was a flat roof that was meant as a garden area for the apartments, and it is quite hidden from where eyes can see—the perfect place for Julian to be hiding!

"JULIAN! I know you're up there! It's getting boring chasing after you now!" I yelled.

He didn't answer, but it was because he didn't answer that I knew he was up there. Usually, pigeons swarmed the roof of his shop; I don't know why, but they were always there. The fact that it was clear meant someone was definitely up there.

I climbed the ladders, and of course, I was right! There he sat, shivering in the corner, whimpering in fear.

"Why do you look so scared?" I asked.

"I never meant to hurt anyone... I know I acted tough, but I just wanted to live in my world so I could have friends and family. I didn't want to kill anyone along the way. I got too entrapped in power!" he sobbed.

I hadn't seen Julian this way before—actually caring about things in the world and about people in the world. But I couldn't tell if he was just trying to trick me. I guess I am trying to trick him either way, so I should probably just play along with it.

"Well, you have the other mirror now, don't you? So, everything will be great for you!" I said.

"No, it didn't work," he muttered.

"What did you say?" I asked.

"I said it didn't work!" he shouted.

"Why didn't it work, though?" I questioned.

"Because I'm not the real Julian... I'm just the Julian of this world, that world, and everything in between. My blood doesn't work," he said.

"Well, can I do anything to help you?" I asked.

"Why would you help me?" he questioned.

"Because I want to help you get your happy ever after," I replied.

"There is only one thing you would be able to do

to help me," he said.

"And what would that be?" I asked.

"Go to the real world and bring me Julian's blood."

"What?! I can't! If you remember correctly, you stole the items I needed to repair the mirror to go back to the other world!"

"Yes, I know, but you're more powerful than a mirror! You can make it back yourself!"

"No, I really can't! The mirror is literally what gives me any kind of power."

"I know, but with every single piece of energy this world has left, you can make it back through!"

"I couldn't even put out the fire at the house!"

"You didn't believe in yourself! You gave up!"

"I don't know how to believe in myself anymore! My family doesn't believe in me; my brother is gone, and the only two friends I had, Jim and the real Julian, I don't have anymore! I've given up on belief at this point, and I just want to get this all over and done with, so we don't have to deal with it anymore."

"Oh well, too bad! You're the only one who can do anything to save us right now! I'm sorry if that's too much of a burden, but get used to it! I could have helped put out that fire that killed Jim, but I didn't, and I will blame myself every day for that, but you're the one who started the fire in the first place, so now you don't get to complain that you don't believe anymore because otherwise, we all disappear to nothing!"

"FINE! Show me how, and I will try my best, but don't expect me to be able to do it!"

He definitely must have been trying to anger me because it was working! I don't believe that I can cross worlds, but if I can...

"Close your eyes," Julian told me.

"How can I trust you're not going to leave me?" I asked.

"Because this time, I need something from you,"

he replied.

"Okay. How will I know if it worked?" I asked.

"Because you won't be in this world anymore," he said.

"Okay, but how will I know I'm not in this world? They look identical," I asked.

"You will just know, okay?!" he shouted, "now close your eyes!"

I shut my eyes, giving way too much trust to Julian, but I had to if I wanted him to trust me.

"Now think about the last place you were in, in that world," he said.

I think the last place I was in was the museum when I was getting the mirror shard.

BRBRBRBRBHRHBHGHGB!

The ground rumbled beneath me once again; whatever Julian was telling me to do was working! The world was giving me its energy to send me through!

"Keep thinking of where you were! Ignore the world collapsing around you! The last thing you're going to want to do is think of something that makes you sad and turn it into a happy thing, giving you the strength to cross through," Julian announced.

I imagined being with Chip again and how happy I would be to hold him in my arms right now. With his soft fur, his silky ears, and his ability to put my mind at ease with just his stare... Then it stopped. The rumbling, the destruction—it all stopped. I opened my eyes, and yes, I was here!

"Owwww! Ahhhhh! AOWWW!" I shrieked.

I was definitely back in the normal world! But for how long?

I was back in the museum again, right where I had disappeared before, although this time it had been days since I had actually arrived.

Now my adventure had begun to find Julian, I left through the doors to the garbage room. I could probably use my power to get through the front door now, but if Julian was still stuck in the hole, then it would probably be best for me to go back the way I came in.

Down the ladder, I went into the sewers. I ventured until I saw if the worst thing that could happen had happened. Julian's legs were dangling down from the hole. I crept over calmly before touching it to see if he was still alive.

"Oi! Who's touching my leg?" he shouted.

"You're alive!" I shrieked.

"Lucas. Is that you? You're alive!?" he asked.

"Yes, of course, I'm alive. I just faded into the other world for a few days. How are you alive should be the question?" I asked.

"There were some old tins of mushy peas and a few bottles of water I've been living off; did you manage to fix the mirror? Is that how you're back?" he asked.

"Mushy peas… ewwwww!" I whined.

"Well, it was that or death, so you know I chose the best option!" he said.

"The best option was death!" I said.

"Okay, did you manage to fix the mirror then?!" he asked angrily.

"Well, no, not exactly," I replied.

"Then how are you here right now?" he asked.

"This is really weird, just talking to your legs," I mentioned.

"Okay! Answer my question! How are you here right now?" he asked again.

"So basically… You in the other world betrayed me and stole all the items to create his own world, but now I'm helping him gather some more items that he didn't get," I said.

"Why…?" Julian asked, confused.

"I don't know, but I need something from you. Your blood... happen to carry any around?" I asked sarcastically.

"What, why, how had this even all happened so quickly?" he asked.

"I couldn't tell you if I wanted to, but you may feel a slight pain in your leg in a second," I said.

"You better not cut my leg! I'll wiggle!" he threatened.

I got a knife out of my pocket that Jim had given me when we were planning on stabbing the other world Julian, although his wiggling around really didn't make it easy.

"Can you just sit still, please?!" I begged.

"You are trying to cut my leg open! I will get an infection and most likely die!" he said.

"Yeah, well, I will hopefully have the mirror fixed soon, and I will help you!" I offered.

"How? You just told me that the other me stole all of the items," he questioned.

"Yes, but I think I have another way!" I said.

"Okay, then what is this other way you speak of?"

he asked.

"I can't tell you just in case it doesn't work... Just please let me get what I need, and I'll get going. Time is limited!" I shouted.

He sat still and didn't say another word; in fact, I didn't even tell him once I had gotten all I needed, as my power had run out. Off I went back to what was left of my world...

As I slowly faded out, I could see the amount of blood pouring out of his leg. He was going to be dead by the time I got back. and I can't do anything about it.

"Lucas!" I heard a faint voice. "Lucas, hello."

Woah... It was different this time coming back to this world; it took a lot longer to get through. It was almost like I was stuck!

"Lucas, I really need you to try getting back to me now!" I heard the other Julian say.

I was trying as hard as I could, but I was stuck! I

couldn't move between the worlds!

"LUCAS! If you don't get back soon, the world will be gone!" he shouted.

But I couldn't... I didn't... I didn't want to. Yeah, that's right! I don't want to go back through!

"Lucas, please. If you can hear me, come through! I know it's painful, but if you don't, then you will never see your family or anyone again! You can save them; you can save everyone!" he stated.

This was what I needed to hear. I know that everything had been going wrong, but for a second, just that split second, one person believed in me. This lit a spark in me that I thought was gone forever.

"AHHHH! OWWWW!" I shrieked, trying to push through the pain.

"Go on, Lucas! You can do it!" he cheered.

"I! AHHH! CAN! AHAHHOWOWOW" DO THIS!" I bellowed.

CRASH! I dropped to the ground, and around me,

the world rumbled to crumbles, racing towards us. Time is running out.

"You've done it, Lucas!" he screeched.

I lied on the floor in pain, slowly trying to get back up.

"Did you get what I needed?" he asked.

I couldn't answer; I felt too weak.

Julian began searching me, looking for the blood, and eventually found it behind me.

"YES, NOW I WILL HAVE MY WORLD!" he shouted.

"Help me…" I stuttered.

"Help you? Why would I do that? You got me what I needed, and I will let you live until the world swallows you whole!" he laughed.

I don't know what I expected, to be honest. The one person who finally put some belief in me had betrayed me **AGAIN!** I still had my plan to trap him between the mirrors, but right now I needed a second to breathe.

"Now all I need to do is cover my mirror in the blood of the other me!" he grinned.

He ripped open the bag I had stored the blood in and dripped it over the mirror until the frame turned red like anger!

"AHHHHH!" he shrieked.

It seems the world has merged completely now! Julian's leg tore open from where I had cut the other Julian's leg! He looked up at the sky and continued to scream louder than anything I had ever heard. His face burned, and his soul left his body. Soon he was ash on the floor, swept away by the wind!

"Julian…" I whimpered.

I leaned up with all my might and looked at where Julian had been sitting, and now there was nothing.

The new mirror began to glow a white glare of light; it began expanding around me until I was submerged within! The energy powered me to be able to stand; in fact, at this point, my feet were no longer touching the ground; I was levitating!

The faces of my enemies began to appear around me, and I began whispering things into my ears, trying to make me weak!

"What are you going to do now?" a voice said.

"Look around you! Your world is nothing!" another said.

Then the laughter began.

"HA HA HA"

"HE HE HE"

"OOOOOH"

"You're such a failure; you couldn't even keep the items that you had found for longer than a day!" a voice said.

They were all right! Everything they said, but you know what? I think I've done pretty well considering I've only been in this town for 13 days!

The voices weren't angering me, which angered

them. I closed my eyes and imagined them gone, but that wasn't all I wanted; I wanted one more conversation with my family, and that is exactly what I got.

"Mum! Dad! Chip! Granny! You're all here!" I shouted in excitement.

"Hey, don't forget about me!" Joe exclaimed.

"JOE!" I shouted.

"Hello, L man!" my dad said.

"Dad… You remember me?" I asked.

"Well, of course!" he said in a confused tone.

I had a smile of happiness and then a frown of disappointment. This wasn't real; this was just me managing to conjure up versions of them that I remembered from when I was really young.

"Luke, just trust in yourself, and it will all work out!" Granny said.

"I miss you, Lukey," Mum said.

"I miss you guys too," I sobbed.

"Lucas, I need to talk to you in private," Granny said.

"Um… Okay… Ghost dead; other family members disappear, I guess," I said, not really knowing how to make them go.

"Lucas, you're not out of time," Granny said.

"What do you mean? I don't know what to do, Granny," I muttered.

"But you do, Lucas! You are the only person left in the world! In the universe!" she said.

"But what if it doesn't work? And I fail all of us?" I asked.

"Well, at least you would have tried, and Lucas, that is the best thing you can do!" she told me.

Every now and then people have a little cry because they are overwhelmed, and now was my time to have a cry. I squeezed my eyes closed, holding back the tears, and hugged my grandmother for what seemed like the first time.

When my eyes opened, I was hugging the air and alone again, but not for long!

I slowly landed back on the ground, the white, glowing beam disappearing around me, and back into the new mirror. Once it was gone, everything was flying around me—bricks, rubble, glass, everything! I grabbed the original mirror to my world from the ground and stared it straight at the other mirror; they both exploded into pieces and grew into each other like power lines. I was struggling to hold it without falling over! I was now standing on the last piece of the world there was left, trying to hold on!

BANG!

The mirror exploded, and I fell back into the darkness of nothingness.

Gone…

Nothing left…

"COME ON, LUKE, WAKE UP!" mum shouted.

Wait what?! I was at home (Granny's house)! What's happening? Did I save us? Had I actually done it? I jumped out of bed and ran down the spiralling staircase to the dining room, where everyone was sitting, gathered around the dining table.

"Come on, eat your breakfast before it gets cold, Luke," my dad said.

"Breakfast? Did I do it then?" I asked.

"Do what? Luke, just eat your food," my mum said.

I sat down and ate my food while receiving weird stares from around the table. I was waiting to see if anyone was going to say anything, but no one did. I did just save the world, I think.

"You guys want to go watch a movie by the fireplace today?" my dad asked.

"A movie? I'm sorry, does nobody remember the last couple of weeks?" I asked.

"What are you talking about, Luke? Why are you acting so weird already?" Joe asked.

"I'm acting weird! You're the ones acting weird!" I shouted.

"Luke, that's enough now!" my dad shouted.

"Where's Granny?" I asked.

If anyone was going to remember, it would be her!

"Luke, don't do this," Mum sighed.

"Do what?" I questioned.

"You know your grandmother is dead!" she stated.

I felt sick to the bottom of my stomach. What does

she mean dead?! This wasn't what I wanted.

"WHAT?!" I shouted.

"Luke, are you okay? Why are you acting like this?!" my dad questioned.

"I need to go out," I said.

"You can't go out. It's Christmas morning!" Mum exclaimed.

"What?! Christmas? You know what? Never mind. I need to go and talk to someone quick," I said.

"Okay, well, at least get changed out of your pyjamas!" Mum told me.

"Okay," I agreed as I ran up the stairs towards Granny's' room.

I wanted to know if the mirror was still there; after all, if it was, Granny would most likely be in that world!

No! It was gone! I had to go see Julian—the real Julian.

I went into what seemed to be my room and threw

on some clothes like Mum had told me to, which was actually rather refreshing considering I hadn't changed in over a week. Then I left straight out of the house and down to his shop!

I ran faster than I had ever run before and arrived in seconds; he was in there alive and well!

"JULIAN!" I shouted in excitement.

"Hey Lucas, How are you doing today?" he asked.

"You remember me?" I asked.

"Well, of course. Are you okay?" he asked.

"You don't know how much of a relief it is to know that someone remembers me and all the other world stuff!" I said.

"Other world?! What are you talking about?" he asked in a worried voice.

"But I thought you knew me," I said.

"Well, yes, I was married to your grandmother," he replied.

"So, you remember then?" I asked.

"No, I don't know what you're talking about?!" he answered.

I couldn't tell what was going on or what I should say. I had just saved two worlds at once, and now no one remembers...

"Do you happen to know of a mirror?" I asked.

"I know of plenty of mirrors... What one are you looking for?" he asked.

"It's the most magnificent piece you would have ever seen; it's got a rather magical feel to it," I said.

"I think I know what you're talking about. I've got it in the window of the shop; help yourself and have a look if you would like," he offered.

I calmly walked out of the shop and turned to the mirror. There it was. Staring me in the eyes after all the pain it had caused! I don't know if I'm in another world now, but I do know I want no part of it!

"Julian, can you get the mirror out for me?" I asked.

"I suppose so," he said.

He pulled the mirror out for me and leaned it against the wall.

"I know this is your store, but would you mind giving me some space?" I asked.

"Um… I really shouldn't leave you here," he said.

"What do you think I'm going to do? Steal?" I asked angrily.

"No, of course not... Of course, I'll give you 5 minutes," he offered.

"Thank you," I replied.

I raised my hand to the touch of the mirror, closed my eyes one last time, and pictured it gone from my life forever! When I opened them, it was still there, in one piece. Nothing happened!

"Goodbye!" I whispered before I smashed my hand into it, making it shatter over the floor.

"AAHHHHHHHHHHHHHHH" screams echoed around.

"Who's the powerful one now?" I laughed.

I had won, finally! Or had I…

Each of the pieces of the mirror reflected a different ending. I still have yet to find mine.

To be continued…

www.ingramcontent.com/pod-product-compliance
Lightning Source LLC
Chambersburg PA
CBHW051136190726
48290CB00006B/1870